MW01517641

# OTHER FICTION

A STRANGER DEAD
A RED DARK NIGHT
APRIL (WRITING AS PETER FOX)
MAGIC MAN (DELUXE CHAPBOOK)
THE WAY OF THE FOG (THE ARK OF LIGHT VOL. 1)
DEVIL'S PLAYGROUND (WITH KEITH GOUVEIA)
ON HELL'S WINGS (WITH KEITH GOUVEIA)
ZOMBIE FIGHT NIGHT: BATTLES OF THE DEAD
MAGIC MAN PLUS 15 TALES OF TERROR
UNDENIABLE
THE DANCE OF MERVO AND FATHER CLOWN
FLASH ATTACK: THRILLING STORIES OF TERROR,
ADVENTURE, AND INTRIGUE

# ANTHOLOGIES (AS EDITOR)

DEAD SCIENCE
ELEMENTS OF THE FANTASTIC
VICIOUS VERSES AND REANIMATED RHYMES: ZANY
ZOMBIE POETRY FOR THE UNDEAD HEAD
METAHUMANS VS THE UNDEAD
BIGFOOT TERROR TALES VOL. 1 (WITH ERIC S. BROWN)
BIGFOOT TERROR TALES VOL. 2 (WITH ERIC S. BROWN)
METAHUMANS VS WEREWOLVES

# NON-FICTION

BOOK MARKETING FOR THE
FINANCIALLY-CHALLENGED AUTHOR
CANADIAN SCRIBBLER: COLLECTED LETTERS OF AN
UNDERGROUND WRITER
LOOK, UP ON THE SCREEN! THE BIG BOOK OF
SUPERHERO MOVIE REVIEWS
GETTING DOWN AND DIGITAL: HOW TO SELF-PUBLISH YOUR
BOOK
THE CANISTER X TRANSMISSION: YEAR ONE
THE CANISTER X TRANSMISSION: YEAR TWO
THE CANISTER X TRANSMISSION: YEAR THREE

## POETRY

The Hand I've Been Dealt
Haunted Melodies and Other Dark Poems
Still About A Girl

**WWW.CANISTERX.COM**

**Flash Attack**

**Thrilling Stories of Terror, Adventure, and Intrigue**

**by**

**A.P. Fuchs**

To Krizan,

Nice meeting you.

Enjoy!! :)

Best, *[signature]*

'22

COSCOM ENTERTAINMENT

WINNIPEG

ISBN 978-1-927339-68-8

Published by Coscom Entertainment

Text set in Garamond
Printed and bound in the USA

This is for Dad.

**Flash Attack**

**Thrilling Stories of Terror, Adventure, and Intrigue**

# Attacked: An Introduction

The following stories started as a challenge to myself as I began Year Three of my weekly newsletter, *The Canister X Transmission*. The plan? Send out one flash fiction story a week, which I did, and which were an assortment of adventures stories, horror stories, superhero stories, and more. I also knew they would eventually be collected in book form in two ways: one, in the collected edition of *The Canister X Transmission: Year Three* and, two, as a separate collection of short-short stories. I also knew I wanted more stories than that which had gone out during Year Three, so I wrote some bonus tales while Year Four got underway. These extra stories are contained here. As well, the stories that had gone out during Year Three will not be exactly the same as their original digital weekly counterparts due to some light editing. So, in a way, the stories contained herein are all new. Sort of.

As an exercise, writing a flash fiction story week-to-week was a good way to keep the writing machine going. After all, each newsletter needed a story as part of its contents. There was no dropping the ball on that one lest I let myself down and my readers down. It was also a chance for me to explore ideas and concepts that might remain as they are presented here, or might serve as premises for future work.

Flash fiction is a tricky beast. Though short and sweet, it's important each story contains a beginning, middle, and an end. Each tale is not simply an excerpt of a greater whole. They are *stories*. Full stories. Just short. The aim is to pack each one with as much entertainment and information as possible, and leave the reader satisfied in the end.

For this collection, no genre was off-limits. Sure, from a marketing perspective, it might have been best—even smarter—to stick to a single genre, but my brain isn't wired that way, and each week my mood fluctuated and a craving to write in one genre would outweigh another. What we have here is a mix, and they are published in the order they were written thus giving you, the reader, a surprise every time you dive into a new tale.

It's my sincerest hope that not only are you entertained by what's to follow, but also your reading habits are expanded by exploring a writing medium that isn't very common. I believe it's important for any reader, myself included, to try new things, so this book is an effort to help with that.

Thank you for taking part, and I welcome you to *Flash Attack: Thrilling Stories of Terror, Adventure, and Intrigue.*

- A.P. Fuchs
Winnipeg, MB
May 20, 2017

# The Key

Reluctantly, he handed over the key.

If only she knew what it was for. But she had no idea. She couldn't have. Not even after all this time. Oh, but when she found out . . .

The thought gave him pause. Could she be trusted? Would she come through? If she was anything, she was honorable. This he knew. But the key, the one he'd been guarding his whole life. Once she had it . . .

It was only a matter of time, he supposed, before he told her. She knew about the key, that was for sure. Knew about it all along, actually, but not what it was for. The plan had been to never tell her its power, but things didn't always go accordingly to plan.

It was after a few nights in the bar that he let the details about the key's power slip. The third night, actually, the one filled with heavy beer and tequila shots. Keeping a filter when under the influence was never his strong suit. Sure, he could do it. Even force it—after many beers he *had* to force it—but eventually the walls came down and he told her about what the key could do.

It opened the door to that other place.

That place he hadn't been to since he was a child.

She was immediately intrigued and, like all good women taking care of drunken men, laughed it off as if he'd simply had drank too much and that was it. But after, when he was sober and made a foolish attempt at covering his tracks, she totally called him on it—had she really known all along?—and learned that the door—that portal—wasn't a thing of fables.

Magic realms were real.

But you needed a key to get to them . . . and he had one.

It was the one he gave her.

And, he knew, he'd only give it to her.

# The Trapeze Artist

She knew she wasn't supposed to, but how else would she star in the greatest show on Earth?

As her feet left the mattress, she reached out and grabbed the invisible trapeze bar in front of her. As her body fell back onto the bed, she imagined gripping it with all her might. Now prone, she pictured herself swinging through the air, heading straight toward another bar coming her way.

Back on her feet, she grabbed the new bar and released the other. Again, a backwards jump and she was sailing.

*Quick! Turn around. That other bar is swinging back to you!* she thought.

She flipped over onto her stomach, the mattress bouncing beneath her. No, not a mattress, just a cushion of air as she took hold of the new bar again.

The rush of wind breezed past her as she swung across the great divide. Quickly, she turned around on the bar, tucked her legs under herself, and rolled through the air, flipping, spinning, arms back out in front of her.

But there was nothing there to grab on to.

She immediately prepped herself for the sensation of freefall as she fell backward toward the safety net below. It absorbed her fall, took her in, nearly wrapped itself around her from her weight, then shot her back up into the air like a slingshot as she was sent to meet the bar. She firmly took hold, then rocked her body back and forth to build up the momentum to swing out again. Her legs folded up in front of her and she let go, did a backflip, and grabbed the other bar and rode it to the safety of the terrifically high trapeze stand.

The surrounding crowd applauded.

She took her bow.

The roar of clapping broke apart until only a lone person slowly clapped for her.

It was her mother, and she didn't look impressed.

## Comics Power

Steve stood there staring at the comic's opening page. It was that giant green robot again, the one that had terrorized Manhattan two months ago, the same one the Cosmic Kid had put an end to. Now it was back and was slamming holes into the bottom of the Empire State Building. It wouldn't be long until the whole structure came toppling down.

He turned the page.

Citizens ran away from the robot in all directions, getting to safety. A military chopper flew overhead, firing bullets into the robot's armored hull.

Useless.

The robot kept punching into the building's walls and supports, working its way around the sides. What its agenda was, Steve didn't know.

On page three, a tank rolled up and fired. The round simply exploded against the robot's back, not fazing it. The military never stood a chance never mind any do-gooder cops that'd come along and try to take the thing down.

"There really is only one option," Steve said.

He turned the page again and blue and red light swirled out and engulfed him in a tornado of power, pulling him directly into the comic book. Now clad in red tights and a blue cape, Steve boldly stood before the robot as the Cosmic Kid. The machine turned its attention on him and made its way toward him.

He had work to do.

## The Choice

If being a starship captain was any one thing, it was about making decisions. Captain Redd Trevor knew as much after serving on the *S.S. Fang* for over twenty years.

And now it had come to this.

The majority of his main crew had been lost when the Starlus boarded. What human could possibly stand a chance against creatures twice their height with insectoid-like shells covering their bodies?

The ship's hallways were painted with blood and torn uniforms. Few of Captain Trevor's extended crew were still alive, most held up in the engineering department and sickbay. From what he could tell, the families on board were mostly dead except for some who had managed to jam the doors to their quarters.

Twenty-four years on the *Fang*.

So many people come and gone.

So many missions.

So many victories and so many close calls.

Now the final call had come and Captain Trevor had to make his choice. A dance of fingers along the console and the self-destruct sequence would be initiated. Destroying the ship wouldn't annihilate the entire Starlus race, but it would remove at least a large portion of them from being a further threat to the cosmos.

But the people on board. No one knew what he was about to do. No one knew their lives were in his hands and were moments away from ending. Yet how many more people or those of other races would die at the hands of the Starlus taking over his ship? If he could at least remove some of their army, it might weaken them for a time. Perhaps, even, weaken them enough so other ships could come in and wage war.

The distress signal had been sent out a long time ago. No other ship was in immediate range.

Those innocent lives . . .

The ship.

The people.

The unknown death in the future.

The choice was clear so why was he afraid?

Perhaps this would be an unforgiveable act, but he would take lives to save them, and it was the saving that was important. It was about the big picture. If destroying the *Fang* would start a war to remove evil from the galaxy, then it was a sacrifice worth making.

Captain Trevor eyed the console . . . and started punching in his code. Once entered, the screen lit up, asking him to confirm.

He thought of those on board. He thought of his crew and even imagined some nodding in approval.

He thought of the families huddled in the corners of their quarters, eyes on the entrances as the Starlus tried to beat down the doors.

The fear.

The faces.

The rapid heartbeats.

His own rapid heartbeat.

Captain Trevor closed his eyes, pressed his finger to the console, then looked at what he'd done.

The countdown began.

A.P. Fuchs

## The Bus

Ted paid the fare on the old transit bus and found a seat about halfway in and next to the window. There were maybe a dozen people on it besides himself.

As the bus got underway and headed to the next stop, a sudden sense of detachment filled Ted's heart and it no longer seemed like he was just another human riding the bus. Sure, he was there, and so were the others . . . but he wasn't one of them.

Could've been all the mistakes he'd made over his life.

Could've been the extra beer he had with breakfast. It *was* his breakfast.

Still, he looked around.

That old guy over there: worn, leathery skin, a scar on his cheek. The man's jaw was a near perfect square and his plaid shirt did little to hide the now-aged and sagging muscle beneath it. It wouldn't have surprised Ted if the old timer was a war vet. Most likely. A lot of old men were.

That woman over there, dark skin, a flowery dress. She smelled of berry-scented perfume and it drifted all the way over. He knew it was a stereotype but he got a quick mental flash of her in the kitchen and guessed when she served you a meal, she served you the equivalent of two under the guise of one.

Or that teenager with the long, scraggly hair hanging out of a baseball hat without a

10

curved peak. He hated it when kids didn't curve their hats. Didn't they know it kept the sun off their face better? The teenager had his eyes glued to his phone. Texting or gaming, Ted didn't know, but he felt bad the younger generation seemed to live their lives through a screen instead of through their own two eyes.

Another teenager, this one a girl, fairly homely, but who was he to judge? He was in his late forties; she was probably around sixteen. He remembered the girls back when he was that age. Had they all looked like that with crooked teeth and a hooked nose? Didn't matter. She seemed sad. He almost wanted to talk to her to ask her what was wrong, but that would've marked him a creep so he stayed in his seat.

Everyone here had a story.

Even the stories he assigned the ones he just looked at, he probably wasn't accurate, but that's what people did: looked and judged. Come up with a nice tale and you could make yourself feel better about someone else without even knowing the truth.

The bus started and stopped, picking people up, letting people off.

The cars passed outside his window.

Humanity on wheels.

And he was here, seated above them on the old transit.

Detached.

## Cotton Candy Pink

When Trevor asked his mom to buy him the latest in neon fashion, he didn't count on her getting him an outfit that made him look like a gumball.

"Pink," he had said. "All pink."

It was a new thing, the guys at school wearing pink. Normally a girl's color, it suddenly became cool for the boys in grade six to have splashes of neon pink somewhere on their clothes. You became instantly awesome if you had that, he observed, and it raised you a peg with the girls as well.

Never one to do only the bare minimum, Trevor wanted to go all out but, also never the one with any money, he had to rely on his mom's wallet to make it happen.

And she came through.

She brought the pink.

Just the wrong kind.

"I'm not wearing that," Trevor said the morning he was expected to wear the new outfit she'd bought him. It was a cotton-candy-pink T-shirt, black track pants with a cotton-candy-pink stripe down the sides, a cotton-candy-pink baseball hat, and a pair of shades, with black frames but cotton-candy-pink arms.

"You darn well are going to wear it," his mother said. "You told me pink, I got you pink. Final sale. This is not going to waste."

"Everyone will laugh at me! I wanted neon pink."

"You said 'pink.' I got you pink. Now get dressed or you can forget rides to baseball this week."

That did it. Trevor's team was clobbering all the others in the league and he was the star pitcher, always getting accolades after each game for throwing them in hard and fast.

Trevor got dressed and didn't bother seeing himself in the mirror before leaving. He also avoided what he knew to be a satisfied—even smug—grin on his mother's face because she got her way.

When he got to school, it suddenly felt like all eyes were on him. It was almost as if he wasn't wearing any clothes at all and was parading around buck naked.

He headed toward the doors to wait for the bell to ring.

"What's up there, little piggy?" Stew called from the four-square painted in yellow on the asphalt.

"You tell me, chunky!" Trevor shot back.

"What did you say?" Stew threw down the basketball, seemingly not caring it bounced several times then rolled off to the side into a crowd of girls. He marched over to Trevor.

Between actually wearing the cotton candy pink and the sudden insult, Trevor couldn't believe what he'd done. Messing with Stew would likely get your face mangled.

"Um . . . hunky?" Trevor said. *Stupid recovery.*

"So, what, you have a thing for me now?" Stew laughed and glanced around. Those within earshot started laughing, too, and soon a crowd started to form around them.

"No. No way."

"You said 'hunky.'" Stew drew out the word and Trevor immediately felt his cheeks flush.

"I said 'chunky'!" He didn't mean to shout it or defend himself so quickly, but there it was, right there out in the open.

"You saying I'm fat now?" Stew didn't waste any time and gave Trevor a shove. The jolt of the impact was harder than Trevor expected.

"No . . . I said . . . um . . ." His legs turned to rubber.

"I'll show you fat," Stew said and moved in with both arms wide as if he was going to give Trevor a bear hug.

Whether it was instinct or not, Trevor knew that "hug" was meant as a takedown. He jumped back a step and Stew missed his grab. Without thinking, Trevor popped him in the mouth. Unfazed, Stew's eyes went wild and he dove in again, this time tackling Trevor around the waist.

The two hit the ground, Stew on top, his weight putting pressure on Trevor's chest, making it difficult to breathe.

"Get off!" Trevor said and smacked Stew again in the mouth. It only made things worse.

Stew grabbed him by the shoulders and pulled him partway off the ground then slammed him back down. The back of Trevor's head hit the asphalt and he fought the sudden burst of black stars that danced across his vision.

He cut loose and punched and punched Stew anywhere he could land his fists. Some hit him in the face, others in the shoulders and chest.

A pair of big hands wrapped around Stew from behind and he was hauled off.

It was the gym teacher, Mr. Matthews.

"Enough!" Mr. Matthews shouted. He tossed Stew to the side as if the heavier kid weighed all of five pounds. He reached down and helped Trevor to his feet. "You okay?"

"Um . . . yeah . . . I guess," Trevor said.

It was then he noticed Mr. Matthews wore a cotton-candy-pink T-shirt, too.

# The Party

"Hold it closer, I can't read it," One said. Though his eyes were adapted to the dark, trying to read the text on the card Two held out for him was still difficult.

"Here, is this better?" Two said.

"Yeah."

There wasn't much light coming into the six-by-eight-foot space, only the little that came through the two-inch-tall space beneath the door. There wasn't anything in here. Just four walls, one of which had the door. A locked door. It had been home to One and Two since as far back as they could remember.

"'Soon you will be free. It will be the party of a lifetime,'" One said, reading the card.

"What do you think it means?"

"I don't know. What is a 'party'? Never heard that word before."

"I think it means seeing a group of people or something."

One studied Two's face: brown hair, brown eyes, blank expression. Apparently One also had brown hair and brown eyes.

"Do you think he'll let us out?" Two asked.

"Mr. Numbers?"

"*Doctor* Numbers," Two said. "You know he hates being called 'Mister.'"

"Right. Not sure what the difference is."

One and Two were the same height—so Two discovered when they stood back-to-back that one time. They also were the same build—thin, but sturdy. They also wore the same clothes—a black jumpsuit which sometimes made Two look like a floating head in the dark.

There was a knock at the door and a voice came from the other side.

"You boys ready?" It was Dr. Numbers.

"For the party?" One asked.

"Yes. A lot of important guests are here."

"Guests?" Two whispered. "What are 'guests'?"

"I guess we'll find out," One said. To the door: "Yes, we are ready."

"Then stand back. I'm opening the door," Dr. Numbers said.

There was a *ka-chunk* and the door opened. Light flooded into the tiny room and One immediately shut his eyes. A moment later, a firm hand pulled on his arm. He guessed it was Dr. Numbers touching him because there was no way Two would grip him so hard. He was slowly guided forward.

He blinked open his eyes.

The room was bright, light seeming to cover everything. People much taller than him stood around in a semi-circle. Some were like him and Two and Dr. Numbers. Others—they looked thinner, smoother, with rounder hips and two balls sticking out of their chests beneath their clothes. They wore really long shirts, ones that ran down to their knees, and their shoes had spikes sticking out of their heels. One didn't know how they could balance on those.

"Ladies and Gentlemen," Dr. Numbers said, "I give you One and Two. Identical in every way and holding the inner properties you are all looking for."

The people slapped their hands together in quick succession. One didn't understand why they did that. He didn't like the noise.

He looked over at Dr. Numbers and took the man in for the first time. He was taller than him, with gray hair, wrinkled skin—skin that wasn't the same color as his own.

Dr. Numbers's skin was lighter, like a very light brown, kind of white.

Two. He glanced over at Two.

Two looked different as well, out here in the light. His hair appeared a lighter brown and his dark skin was a different color, one that reminded him of the plum Dr. Numbers had given them that one time.

"Now, now, don't be shy," Dr. Numbers said.

One wasn't sure if the man was talking to the people or to him and Two.

The people closed in, and the next thing One knew, him and Two had hands running all over them, feeling their faces and their bodies through their clothes.

One overheard someone say to Dr. Numbers, "You sure you bred them properly?"

"Yes," Dr. Numbers replied quietly. "Isolated in the dark as instructed. They're ready for sampling."

"Excellent," the other person said.

Two leaned in and whispered to One, "Do you know what 'sampling' means?"

One was surprised Two heard the exchange, but then again, each of their hearing seemed to be the same: nice and sharp. "I think that's the first game of the party."

"Good. I'm excited."

Dr. Numbers stepped between One and Two and put his arms around each of their shoulders. "Boys, are you ready?"

"Yes," One said.

"Uh huh," Two said.

"Good." To everyone else: "Are you ready?"

Smiles lit the room and each person produced a couple of small, shiny objects.

One recognized them as knives and forks from a picture book he once looked at in that small room.

The people stepped closer.

Knives drawn.

# The Split

It was her picture that always got to him, and tonight was no different.

Gabriel stood before the picture of Valerie on the nightstand beside his bed. He picked it up, held it—almost as if he was holding *her*. She was everything. Brown hair, brown eyes, forceful yet tender, and that little smile that said, "I know something you don't."

He wondered if that little something was that she loved him as much as he loved her.

He looked down at himself: he wore his Axiom-man uniform—dark blue tights with a light blue cape, light blue gloves, and a light blue stretch of tough fabric that ran diagonally across his chest.

Like the tough fabric over his heart.

He hadn't put the mask on yet, one of the many he wore. One of them, his glasses, were on the nightstand, too.

Should he let her in? *Completely* let her in?

Valerie wasn't just some girl he knew. She represented what life could be—a home, a family, someone to love each and every day.

The costume he wore was something else.

The costume wasn't a warm home filled with Thanksgiving and Christmas dinners, a mowed lawn, and a small pool in the backyard.

It was a symbol of truth and hope for a city that was barely hanging on. It was light in a dark place yet also a light slowly being consumed by the shadows and filth that coated Winnipeg's streets.

Deep down, Gabriel knew he couldn't have it both ways.

While it was true both paths led to a better place, one certainly outweighed the other.

Valerie was about her, himself, and those they'd influence through family and friends.

Being Axiom-man . . . that was about impacting the city, even the world, and pointing the way to a life where crime and war and evil weren't common.

But there was a cost. He'd have to leave Valerie alone. He'd have to leave *himself* alone, that part of him deep down that yearned for normalcy and love and care and a person to live for.

Split.

Despite all he could do, despite all the good he'd done thus far, he just didn't know if he had the strength to keep it up.

Every time he set himself aside to help others, a little piece of him went missing. Now . . . now he was able to feel it—the hollowness inside, as if his heart no longer beat with blood and passion but with cold duty and obligation.

He didn't want that.

Becoming Axiom-man had been a choice he made because he couldn't look the other way while others suffered.

But now . . .

Would the battle ever end?

Would he ever be in a position to choose between Valerie and the rest of the world and no matter what choice he made it would end up being the right one?

His heart ached for her.

But it also ached for those outside, right now, on the street.

Those that needed his help.

He set the picture down.

Gabriel fixed his mask in place and activated his powers.

Valerie would have to wait.

## Sniper

*Those dumb bastards,* I thought. *They can barely walk, and never mind about them talking. One leg dragging behind the other. Must've been a hell of a bar night.* I sniffed. *As if that's the case here.*

I paused and was dismayed to find myself laughing at my own lame jokes. Was that what I had come to? Some horrible, self-entertaining comedian?

I lined up the rifle at the guy shuffling down the street. Well, "shuffling" wasn't the right way to describe his walk. He used his right leg to pull the rest of his body forward as he made his way down the sidewalk, just like the guy some dozen feet behind him.

*Brain dead, is what they are. All of them. Yet . . . there's got to be something rattling around upstairs. How else could you walk?* I leaned against the window sill. The glass that once covered it had been knocked out a long time ago. I was on the second floor of a warehouse, an old blue jean factory by the looks of it, what with some denim laying in the dust here and there on the floor. Yet judging by the stacks of boxes and crates all over the place, it seemed it went from jean factory to storage at some point. Storage for what, who knew? *And I don't have time to look through everything, not with Captain Rotten down there almost within shooting distance.*

I lined up my shot but would have to wait roughly another minute for the walking dead man below to get close enough for me to peg him between the eyes.

I could shoot a rifle just like any idiot who knew how to pull a trigger, but my aim wasn't that good at far distances. Then, really, whose was? That stuff you saw on TV, it ain't real. Once heard someone refer to them as "improbably headshots." Totally true. Though I hate guns, they do take skill if you want to consistently hit your mark.

Captain Rotten got closer. Now I could see a chunk of his face was missing . . . or maybe it was just the way his baseball hat cast a shadow on his face. Hard to say. His jaw just kind of hung there slack, as if he tasted something but couldn't quite get that invisible burger into his mouth.

He pulled himself forward, one step, two.

Slow.

I waited, staring down the barrel, finger on the trigger.

I kept him in my sights the whole time and thought what had this world come to? Where was everybody? Were those two walking dead guys out there representatives of the entire human race? If so, then maybe I was the only one left.

*But you've always been the only one,* I thought. Or so it always felt like it. Just me in a sea of zombies. It started with those blasted cellphones. Sorry, "smart" phones. Everyone pretty much zoned out after that.

One step, two. Captain Rotten got closer.

I made sure the end of the barrel kept in line with that sweet spot between his eyes.

Another few seconds and I'd nail him, then I'd get the guy coming up behind him not long after.

Closer.

Captain Rotten had something in his hand. Looked like a mittful of meat.

I took my shot.

## Process

It really wasn't all that difficult—writing.

Peter couldn't figure out why other writers turned making a book into a highly-stressful and unnecessary process of software, hardware, semantics, research, half-glasses, indoor scarves, cardigans with elbow patches, and turtlenecks. Heck, walking into his local bookstore and checking out all the author photos on the wall was like looking at a mosaic of the same person. Different faces, sure, but each man or woman wore the aforementioned writer's outfit and had their head resting on their hand as if in deep thought. So many writer blogs detailed the angst of process and how various programs and tools were required to get a story on paper.

Men and women writers alike—all the same.

Whatever happened to just sitting down at a damn typewriter, plugging in a page, and putting one word in front of the other until the scene was over? Whatever happened to letting the story tell itself?

Peter looked at his own typewriter. The finger outlets were ready as was the head plug.

He took the head plug and inserted its forked end into the metal receptacle in the middle of his forehead. He then put his fingers into the holes along the bottom rim of the key rows and let the small, fine needles within bury themselves into his fingertips. He double-checked the stack of paper behind the typewriter to ensure he had enough for the work to come. Once a page was complete, a new one would automatically feed into the roll while the other tumbled out the top and piled itself just beyond the stack of blank paper.

Clearing his mind, he chased away the events of the day then brought up a mental image of the next scene: Sir Roland on his mighty steed, sword drawn, ready to ride off to save Princess Valia from the evil duke holding her captive.

He knew the image transferred from his mind into his hands when a warm current of electricity ran from his brain down his spine and through his shoulders and arms into his fingertips. The keys began to move one at a time on their own.

*Clak clak. Clakkity clak clak.*

Just one word in front of the other until the scene was over.

It really wasn't all that difficult—writing.

# Andy

Let me tell you about Andy.

Andy has a secret, and I'm not talking about a he's-got-a-few-thousand-bucks-hidden-under-his-mattress one.

He's fairly unassuming, to be sure. Black hair, blue eyes. He's around five-foot-ten-or-eleven, average build (so far as I can see, anyway, though I've never seen the guy with his shirt off). He says he works the assembly line at a kitchen cabinet place. Goes to work, comes home, feeds the dog, falls asleep most nights watching TV.

Again, so he says.

But two weeks ago he and I were downtown grabbing a late-night beer. Andy doesn't drink. I had my Fort Garry Dark; he had a Coke. I had two Darks, in fact. He just stuck with the one Coke.

It was when the UFC match on the big screen behind us suddenly switched over to a hotel fire not far from the pub we were at that let on Andy wasn't what he seemed. He immediately turned around in his chair, eyes glued to the set, and he and I both watched as it was reported the top three floors were ablaze and people were trapped. Below, at the foot of the hotel, firetrucks and emergency workers were already on the scene. You couldn't quite see what they were doing from the camera angle but it was clear they were working out a plan.

I looked at Andy. His eyes were glazed with tears and I knew he couldn't stand to see helpless innocents in a place where at any moment they'd be burned alive.

Andy looked over to me, glanced down at my beer and told me to finish up while he went to the restroom. I wasn't sure what to say other than, "Okay," and watched as he headed to the back of the pub and turned the corner to where the bathrooms were. I've been to those bathrooms and knew at the end of the hall there was a back door.

I looked to the TV set and about ten seconds later, a green human-shaped blur flew in and crashed through the hotel's fiery windows. One by one a man in a mask wearing a green and gray bodysuit flew the trapped people down to ground level.

The flying man had black hair.

No one knew his name and no one had coined one for him.

I looked at Andy's Coke.

I looked at my beer.

I looked back up at the screen and saw numerous people had been rescued and the flying man was gone.

Less than half a minute later, Andy made his way back to our table. He said he was tired and we should probably call it a night because he had to get up early for work.

We paid our bill; Andy picked up the tip.

He and I parted ways just outside the pub's door, and as he turned to head to his car, I noticed a smudge of ash on the back of his neck.

Andy had a secret.

## Old Man Henry

*Look at him. Old and useless*, Ray thought as he watched old man Henry sift through the toolbox. The old geezer must've sorted those tape measures ten times today.

Ray and Dan were helping the old guy frame a house. It was slow-going; only four sections of wall had been put up and they should've been up to at least seven. Another lay on the floor, ready to go. Just had to lift it into position before locking it down.

"These things are a bastard to lift," Dan said.

"No kidding," Ray replied. He and Dan were both twenty-two, gym rats, with V-torsos, tight pecs, and well-muscled arms to show for it.

Yet these walls were killing them.

Ray didn't understand it. He could bench two and a quarter, deadlift three hundred, and shoulder press one-seventy-five. But even then, he still saw stars on one of the lifts as they hoisted the thing up. He didn't tell Dan, though. Dan would never let him live it down.

He caught old man Henry eyeing him.

*What does he want? All he does is sort tools and hand us what we need when we need it.*

Henry had been at the framing game for most of his life. The old guy was in his seventies now and probably would never retire. He did look pretty solid, though.

"You boys better get that wall up before quittin' time," Henry said. His voice was soft, tired, yet had a subtle edge.

"Whatever you say, old man," Ray muttered. *Let's see you lift this.*

He sighed. The sun was brutal and the heat was getting to him. Just one more lift, some nails, a couple braces, and they'd be done for the day.

"Better get this done," Dan said. "I'm sick of these ten-hour days." He shook his head. "This job sucks."

"Yup," Ray said.

They each got into position on either end of what would be the top of the wall when it stood upright.

Ray got his fingers under the top plate.

"Be careful, boys," Henry said.

"Yeah, yeah," Ray said.

He gripped the top plate and squatted down, getting ready. "On three."

Dan got into position and nodded.

"One. Two. Three."

The boys lifted and took the wall to waist height. Ray had to adjust his grip so he could get his hands under it to press it up and start walking it forward.

The moment Ray adjusted his hands, the true weight of the wall sank in and he grunted as he started pressing against it. Green stars burst before his eyes and blackness rimmed his vision while his muscles screamed.

He started to push the wall up and . . .

A loud voice filled his ears but he couldn't make out the words. Something hard was beneath him. Strips of beige ran across his vision.

He knew what those strips were but couldn't think of their name.

The voice took on coherency: "Ray! Get out!"

What? Who?

Ray's head spun and this guy who he knew but didn't know told him, "You're under it. I can't hold it!"

The beige strips suddenly grew bigger as they came crashing toward him.

The quick thought of all going black filled Ray's mind before the beige strips suddenly stopped.

"Pull him out," he heard a gruff voice say.

Something gripped his legs and as he was pulled along the floorboards, he realized it was Dan who yanked on his ankles.

Ray rolled over onto his stomach then watched as old man Henry held the wall by himself with little effort.

He gently set the wall down; it barely made a sound as it touched the floorboards. It was like laying a quilt on a mattress.

"Dude, what happened?" Dan said.

"He blacked out," Henry said, turning around. "It's this damn heat." To Ray: "You all right, son?"

Ray couldn't form the words.

Henry gave him a hard pat on the chest, nearly winding him.

The power.

"You'll be all right," Henry said, and with that, he was back at the toolbox, sorting tape measures for the tenth time that day. "Welcome to my gym."

## Chicken Back of Alley

Gazing into puddle, dirt on outside edge, me see me not me. On knees. Me gray. Skin peeling off skin, rubbing off on chubby fingers. Me can't help it. Don't know what happened. Thoughts broken in pieces. Don't remember.

Me stand and walk around corner to behind building. Me walk slow, foot dragging ground along with me, ankle turned in like broken. Drool and goo drip off chin but arm raise to slowly wipe away. It's dark here.

Back alley.

Stomach growls like mad dog. Me want chicken. But chicken no here. Markets closed at night. Down alley me go. Takes long time to move few feet. Ten minutes for ten paces. Head sore like headache. Don't know what headache is. Hungry.

Turn corner to go behind other building. Street damp like puddle that showed dead man earlier. Hear sound. Sound like girl, with mouth muffled by hand or scarf.

Me see girl now. Man has hand over girl's mouth. Me was right. Hear me not. Me breathe quiet. Me steps too slow to hear on ground. Man wears tall hat and dark cape. Girl wears red dress. Bonnet on cobbles.

Girl's eyes see me. Hand of me reaches up. Takes time. Girls can taste like chicken. Me not sure. Me don't remember.

Man still has back to me. Has knife in hand. He has ring on finger in shape of star. Five points on star. Shiny.

His hand rises like lightning, tearing throat off girl. Feet dragging, me moving slow, me see blood gush from throat over man's hand. Falls down fast, does girl, hard, hits head on floor. Man jumps on her. Me run but really me dragging feet. Me clothes is ripped. Me sleeve also ripped. Teeth marks in arm. Ow, me think.

Me fine.

Man stops what he's doing. Looks up. Sees me. Packs up things and runs past me. Still has knife in hand covered in glove. Knife slides along me neck. Man gone.

Back on knees, me face new puddle. Me eyes droop and left one seems to leak from head. More skin falls. Girl lies on dirty street not far away. Me neck running warm water. Crawling along ground to girl, wanting chicken, licking lips. She stares at me, mouth open.

Crawl on ground takes all night before me reach her. Me smell her drying blood and lick some off her neck. Girl's body is spilled open and entrails decorate red dress like tinsel. They taste like chicken. Taste good.

Neck drips thick blood from me. Hits ground in globs. Me lick it.

Out on street, people walk. Hear them. A whistle blows. Footfalls on cobbles.

Police.

Me dead. Me try to crawl away. They too fast. Me pretend to be like her. Dead.

Me like chicken.

# Woodchips Stirring

Daniel had bought Shelly the gerbil for two reasons. One, it was their six-month anniversary. Two, he felt sorry for it. No one wanted it because of how ugly it was.

Shelly had named the gerbil Befriend because that's what she and Daniel had been before they started dating: best friends.

Befriend was small, fitting into the palm of your hand perfectly, with light tufts of beige fur around its neck, nearly hiding her tiny face. Her body, however, looked as if it had been doused in oil, its golden fur matted in clumps, a deep tan color.

Daniel had also bought Befriend a cage but, when assembling it, he accidentally broke the door. He told Shelly not to worry as he would replace it when he came by tomorrow.

It was night and Shelly was in bed. Eyes closed, the last thing she heard before falling asleep was Befriend squeaking in her cage and moving amongst the woodchips.

Shelly dreamed she was in Befriend's cage with her, wandering along the woodchips like a child in an amusement park. Befriend was nowhere to be seen.

*Hiding in the woodchips,* Shelly assumed.

Just then, her mouth filled with the sensation of fur; her tongue rubbed against the roof of her mouth, trying to work the hair off. She gagged, then spat, and thought it was nothing. She knew she was dreaming and strange things happened in dreams.

A sharp pang hit her throat, a lump somewhere in her esophagus, soft and spongy. It worked its way down. Shelly swallowed, forcing the lump down.

She cleared her throat. "Befriend? Where are you, girl?"

There was a stirring in the woodchips. Then there was a stirring in her stomach.

A prick, like a needle puncturing the inside of her stomach, suddenly caused her to stop moving.

"Ooie," she said. "Ooie" was her word for "ouch."

The prick came again and so did a sharp scraping, something tearing at the interior lining of her stomach. And it wasn't just one sharp scrape—it was two, like two tiny nail heads scratching her internally.

Shelly fell to her knees, the pain red in her imagination, her eyes blurring over with tears. "Ooie."

She put her hands to her stomach and felt something moving within. The coppery taste of blood filled her mouth. The scratching increased. She heard her stomach tearing inside her head.

Then it stopped.

She breathed a sigh of relief and fell to her side.

The scratching resumed and soon the movement in her stomach spread, the lump moving deeper into her, in between the muscles and organs, poking and pricking, ripping her insides to lace. Blood bubbled from her mouth.

The woodchips stirred and her mind quickly focused on Befriend. The woodchips ruffled and Befriend poked her tiny head out of the woodchips. In the real world, the gerbil tore through Shelly's stomach and crawled down her belly, descending lower.

## Shedding the Skin

It had been living inside him for so long that it didn't know if it could break free. His body was its home. But, it had come to this place before, the time to shed the old skin and find a new, younger host. It was a lion; its name, as dubbed by the press, Beast of Night. Beast lived in the body of Herman Gordes. But it wasn't much of a body anymore. Herman was a paraplegic, his neck having been broken when Beast tangled with the swamp monster of Spirits Swamp a long time ago.

Before, on the nights when the Northern Lights danced like wisps of bright cloud on a chalkboard, coming out of Herman was easy. Now, coming out was difficult as Herman, having resigned to being a seventy-two-year-old man in a wheelchair, had stopped feeding Beast the anger needed to be released.

Beast was on his own. These past few months when the Northern Lights graced the sky, Beast could feel them, sense them, hear them call. But Herman, unbeknownst to himself, would keep the lion contained.

It was time to break free.

Here, inside this body, there was darkness. The only light that came in was when it was day, the sun's rays shining through Herman's old flesh in an odd array of oranges and reds while he was out in his

41

wheelchair, his nurse having taken his shirt off so he could get some sun.

It was night now and Beast had no light to guide him in his task.

*I'm leaving,* Beast told Herman.

Herman gurgled something in his sleep. That was all.

*Goodbye.*

Forepaws pressing against Herman's ribcage, Beast let his claws break free. They punctured the flesh and a spurt of blood splashed Beast in the face. He didn't mind. It fueled him to dig further. Herman awoke and Beast felt him trying to find the strength to scream. He didn't want his friend to suffer. Quickly, he scraped away Herman's lungs, the flesh leaking down the interior of the rib cage like oil on a wall.

Bone. There was bone in the way. Beast brought his paws back then thrust them forward, his claws poking through the gaps in the ribcage and through the muscle and skin on the other side. For the first time ever, his claws probed the air of Herman's bedroom. He curled his paws, the pads finding purchase on Herman's rib bones.

Beast pulled and the bones tore apart, snapping like dried twigs, blood splashing as high as the ceiling. Like a dead man rising from the grave, Beast rose from Herman's body. His friend lay there, his chest a messy heap of skin and bone and flesh, ripped and torn in pink and red folds.

Beast blinked his eyes and saw the world for the first time in years. Tonight he would find a new host.

# If Only You Didn't Yell at Me

He comes out from the bathroom that is adjoined to the master bedroom and sits down on the bed. With shaky fingers, he picks up the photograph of his wife from the night table. She is so beautiful, all dimples and blue eyes. He smiles at her, and when his eyes begin to water, he sets the picture back down.

"If you only didn't yell at me," he says, looking at the blood on his hands then at the woman in the bathtub across the way, "none of this would have happened."

## Getting to be that Time

"Do you think they'll show?" Roger said.

"They're bound to," Mr. Whithers replied.

The two sat on Mr. Whithers's porch, each on old wooden rocking chairs. The chairs, Roger assumed, were probably as old at Mr. Whithers himself. What Mr. Whithers's first name was, Roger didn't know. The old man was forty-two years his senior and he thought it'd be impolite to ask. And he'd thought that for the past four years.

Roger took a sip of his Corona. He looked out onto the lawn in front of the property. The green grass had been steadily turning gray the more the sun went down behind the overcast above them.

"Why do we have to wait for them again?" Roger asked. "Why can't we just h—"

"Part of procedure," the old man replied. "And you ask that every time."

*Every time for the past four years*, Roger thought.

The clouds above eventually began to break; the sun peeked over the horizon. The gray grass took on a shade of orange in places, still gray in others.

Sunset was strange out here on Ferry Road, about fifty miles from the city.

Mr. Whithers's house was the only old farm house left standing on this street. The others had rotted away over time. The nearest neighbors were so far down Ferry they were out of eyeshot.

Roger stood when he thought he saw a glint of light way down the road. "I think that's them." He got up from the chair and went down the porch steps and out onto the front of the property.

The sun was a mere sliver on the horizon.

The moon was somewhere behind one of the few remaining clouds overhead.

In the distance, the glint of light grew bigger, a sparkling diamond against the dark of the road. Soon, the diamond would split into two as each headlight grew more visible.

The sun finally dipped below the horizon.

The bright of the moon glowed behind a cloud, one that reminded Roger of the shape of a paw.

Fitting.

The diamonds broke as predicted and soon two of them drew nearer the property.

Roger was about to turn to tell Mr. Whithers but the old man was already beside him.

Quick.

It was getting to be that time.

As the car drew nearer, Rogers ears picked up the cracking of bone and the tearing of cloth. He glanced over at the old man.

Mr. Whithers was bent over at the waist, his shoulder blades twisting and snapping as the bones inside realigned themselves. His silver hair grew out past his shoulders and his cheeks sprouted thick matts of fur. The old man's face cracked as his nose disjointed and his jaw jut out to near double its length.

Roger's body locked up as the change came upon him, too.

The moon above shone full and bright, and Roger's hands gripped and clawed at the air while his fingers popped as knuckles burst to accommodate their new formation. His knees snapped as the surrounding muscles grew and repositioned themselves. His jeans tore as did his T-shirt. Each thick hair growing from his normally-clean-shaven face pricked like pins through his skin.

Every. Single. One.

He growled at their onslaught, his gums bleeding as his teeth elongated into fangs.

His cheekbones cracked and a blast of hot pain overtook him for a moment. He swooned.

The pain passed.

Those diamonds down the road were spotlights now.

Somewhere in the back of the black van coming down Ferry Road was dinner: the runaways and homeless.

They could always count on the Delivery Man.

Roger and Mr. Whithers howled at the moon, stomachs growling. Together, they tore off down the road, running on all fours.

It was getting to be that time.

# Four

What people didn't know about Titus was that he used to have four million dollars.

Cash.

"The four million-dollar man" he used to call himself. Hitting five million had been the next goal.

It didn't take much to make a million dollars, and took even less effort to make three more million on top of that once he knew what he was doing. All it took were cash deals flipping houses, a few back alley drops for illicit substances, hiring for little and profiting a lot, and minimal tax claims so the government knew he was working but not the specifics. Throw in a few B and Es for sport where the cash would be kept and the goods pawned or sold, hitting four million happened fairly quickly. Took him about seven years. Would've been quicker had he invested the money, but that would leave a trail and create a few headaches so why bother?

No family.

Didn't need one.

Families cost money.

So did friends. Didn't have those either.

Titus lived poor—old, small house; coupons; dollar menu items; thrift store clothes; home garden; anything to save a buck—and lined the walls of his 1908 character home with stacks of hundreds, fifties, and twenties.

He had thought about stripping the place of the copper wiring—copper was worth something, after all—but out of all his fix-it capabilities, electrician wasn't one of them and the cost of the new wiring and labor wasn't worth the reward.

It didn't take much to set the character home ablaze. Some short in the wire after start-up from a blackout and soon the walls were going. They were too hot by the time he tried to smash up the drywall and rescue his cash.

Four. Million. Dollars.

Gone up in flames.

The house had been in shambles prior to the blaze and wasn't worth much. He cleared around sixty grand in insurance money when all was said and done. The money lasted a little while but was quickly spent on overpriced rent, alcohol, and gambling binges for an attempted quick rebuild of wealth.

Now there was nothing.

All Titus had to his name was the pocketful of change from standing on the curb at stoplights with a cardboard sign that read: SPARE ANYTHING? HAVE A NICE DAY.

Cars went by, fancy ones, plain ones. Old trucks and new trucks. Each person behind the wheel clearly content with their vehicle. Maybe even their life. They had *something*. A job or a supportive significant other as evidenced by their car.

Titus longed to have that sense of security again, but after losing everything, he barely had the strength to roll out from beneath the bus benches he found himself sleeping under.

Those people in those cars had something, even simply something to sit on. All he had was a pocketful of change and rubbery, scarred hands from trying to smash the flame-covered drywall with his fists.

Four million dollars.

Titus reached into his pocket and pulled out the day's take: four dollars in quarters, dimes, and nickels.

But today, that four bucks felt like four million.

He could get a cheap sandwich and a coffee; his first meal in two days.

For so long he couldn't get over losing all those bills, nightmares haunted with images of fiery hundreds and fifties, and burning fingers as he smashed into the drywall only to pull out fistfuls of ash.

He figured God had a twisted sense of humor, letting him get burned now instead of later.

That four dollars.

The change in his hand suddenly felt heavier.

Four bucks to get a meal.

Four bucks to eat like a king though being a pauper.

A street king.

Four bucks.

## Tendrils

Roy Blake yanked his ankle free from the alien's slimy tendril as he crawled through the vent of the starship *Edge*. How the thing got on board or what specific species it was, he didn't know. All he knew was he'd been doing a routine systems check in engineering when the thirteen-foot, black-scaled monster with tendrils for arms materialized and started to attack everybody. It took all of thirty seconds and the beast whipped its fifteen-foot-long tendrils around like slimy blades and captured—then ate the heads off—every member of his engineering crew. Some of the bodies were swallowed whole.

Roy was lucky to dive into an escape hatch which, a few feet in, had access to the venting system.

He couldn't let the thing take the ship. He tried communicating with the bridge but the comms were down. The alien must've destroyed the communications panel, perhaps intentionally. Now the thing was in the venting tubes with him. He heard it slap its greasy tendrils against the vent's metallic interior and its scaly body scrape itself along, trying to catch him.

Roy was unarmed.

All he could do was crawl, and sometimes drag, himself until he got to a vent opening so he could get out and run.

He had the layout of the ship committed to memory. He should be coming up on sickbay soon.

The tendrils slapped behind him.

Drag.

Roy picked up his pace though he didn't think he could go any faster scrambling on his hands and knees. His shoulders and thighs burned from the exertion. He'd known for a long time he was out of shape and now he was paying for it.

He'd pay with his life if he wasn't careful.

The thing hissed behind him. It sounded so close. He dared not look back over his shoulder lest he inadvertently slow himself down.

Slap. Drag.

Roy crawled on.

*Go faster. Hurry.* He gave it all he had.

That vent opening should be coming up on the right soon. *Oh please, let it be soon.*

Slap. Slap. Drag.

Slap. Drag.

Roy's legs burned so badly he started to slow down without meaning to.

Hiss.

*Come on!*

A tendril slapped against his heel. He jerked his foot away.

*Push!* He kicked on the speed and for a second it felt like he galloped on hands and knees. His wrist suddenly bent inward and he face-planted against the vent floor. His head swam from the impact and blood trickled from his nose.

Slap. Drag.

The alien had his ankle again; the tendril snaked up his calf and locked on behind his knee. With a violent jerk, it yanked Roy backward.

Screaming as what could only be teeth engulfing his leg, Roy tried to break free even if it meant losing that leg from the knee down.

But the thing had him.

Slap. Drag.

Like a snake slowly enveloping its prey, Roy was pulled backward.

In a moment, he'd be inside it.

## Heavy

Mike gave Steve the ol' one-two.

The guy had it coming after what he pulled. Blindsiding him at the poker table last week cost Steve everything: house, car, life savings. It was supposed to be the bet to end all bets. Early retirement. But Steve cheated. Card up his sleeve or a fixed deck or something.

Quick! Hook to the kidneys. Mike's knuckles sang on impact and he knew he got him good.

Fast shot to the neck to cut off his breathing. A couple well-placed straight punches to the ribs ensured Steve would be winded and would either go down or just stand there and take it the whole time.

Mike clocked him across the jaw, right then left. He came around from behind and struck Steve in the back of the head. He dipped low and hoped an uppercut would finish him off.

But Steve didn't go down. Just stood there, swaying.

Mike went in with another one-two, jerking Steve back. Then again to the kidneys and ribcage. Right, right, left, left, straight.

A couple jabs and another blast to Steve's face.

Mike ended it with another hook to the side of Steve's said, sending him rattling.

Standing there, panting, catching his breath, Mike slipped off the bag gloves and stepped past the masking tape on the heavy bag. On it, in red writing, it said: STEVE.

The guy wouldn't know what hit him.

# Descent

It wouldn't take much.

A bottle of Advil and three quarters of a litre of bourbon and Jack'd be done.

He didn't know if he was going crazy. He just knew he'd made a fair mess of things and there wasn't a piece of him left inside to stand.

He looked at the bottle of painkillers. Looked at the bottle of bourbon. Looked at the Swiss Army knife beside them.

*Just cut the wrists and be done with it*, he thought. *It's faster.*

No job. No more family. He had friends on the periphery who'd have no concept of what it was like to break to the point of no repair.

He was alone.

Always alone.

Heart aching, he reached for the bourbon and took a long, hard swig. You were supposed to sip it. Not tonight. Not here in the shadows of this dingy apartment. Hell, even the streetlights outside had gone out. It was just him.

And the dark.

And the despair.

Jack picked up the knife and gently ran the open blade vertically down his wrists.

*Don't be a pussy. At least make a scratch.* He dug the knife in deeper, this time drawing blood but not hard enough to cut through anything vital.

The knife dropped from his trembling hands and hit the carpet by his feet.

The Advil.

He picked up the bottle and popped off the lid.

*Just suck 'em back a handful at a time*, he thought.

Jack took another shot of bourbon.

Then another.

And another.

He threw a half dozen pills into his mouth and washed them down with a burning mouthful of booze.

*Don't go partway. Do all of it.* His heart raced.

The Grim Reaper looked him in the eye. Who was going to flinch first? The thing's shadowy form stared him down.

"You or me?" the Reaper said.

The Reaper was right: Jack could control this. He could decide when his time was up or the Reaper could. Either way, he knew he was going to die tonight. It just had to be on his terms. His terms. At least this once. At least this one time he could have control. No more bowing to others. No more giving in to the pressure of what you should or should not do.

Jack put another handful of painkillers in his mouth and let them sit on his tongue.

It was him or the Reaper.

He eyed the hooded figure.

And swallowed.

# Guardian

"Wait until King Goldmane hears of this!" Harry said, though he wasn't sure if he would live long enough to report the incident. As a gray hare and backed up against a rough semi-circle of trees, he was running out of options.

"Oh, trust me," Silvernine said, "you will be dead before those long ears of yours will make it into the vicinity of Goldmane's domain."

Harry looked up at the tundra wolf and feared the towering furry beast before him. His nose began to twitch.

"I see you trembling," Silvernine said. "I like seeing that up here in the North."

North. Silvernine was right. Harry was too far from King Goldmane's jurisdiction for the king to do anything about what was going on. He couldn't let Silvernine know he had him there, though.

"Please, I beg you, let me go," Harry said.

"You cross into my realm, into my forest, onto my snow, and expect to live?" Silvernine's eyes narrowed. "Silly rabbit."

"I'm not a rabbit. I'm a hare."

"Tastes the same to me." Silvernine drooled then turned his head away as if out of embarrassment. He turned back, the drool still leaking from his lips. "Now relax. This won't hurt a bit."

Harry looked side to side. There. In between the two trees just to his left. He could squeeze through and lose Silvernine while the tundra wolf negotiated around them. But his legs were frozen from fear and he didn't know if he had the strength to make good on his hopeful escape.

But he had to.

Gathering his resolve, he dug deep and gave it all he had and took off for the two trees. Silvernine was immediately in hot pursuit.

*Run!* Harry told himself.

Silvernine snapped and growled behind him.

Harry dove between the two trees and burst out the other side. He heard Silvernine's enormous paws pound on the crunchy snow, rip into it for a second as he went around the trees, then pound on it again.

"Get back here!" Silvernine shouted.

Harry was going to cry, "Never!" but instead whimpered without meaning to.

Silvernine's thunderous run grew louder. The wolf had longer legs and almost matching agility. Harry scooted left then right then under a skeletal bush, then right, then straight. Silvernine's footfalls died off a moment then vanished altogether.

Harry ran, and when silence gripped the air, he slowed down and stopped just short of the forest's edge. "A little farther." But he was out of breath and his legs were weak from the adrenaline and exertion.

He hopped closer to the forest's edge and when he was just about at the clearing, Silvernine jumped out in front of him.

"You're not leaving, are you?" the wolf asked.

Harry's teeth chattered as he trembled.

Silvernine snarled, teeth bare, more drool. He bowed, about to lunge, when a roar shook Harry to the core and a golden blur sprang out of seeming thin air and pounced on the wolf. Harry glanced over and saw his lion king tear out Silvernine's throat in a gush of flesh and blood. Silvernine's limp body lay on the crimson snow and King Goldmane roared into the frosty air. He shot a look at Harry with wild eyes, fangs at full reveal, dripping blood. He growled a low rumble . . . then his expression softened and his eyes grew warm.

"M-my . . . king," Harry said.

"Lo, I am with you always," the king said.

# Warning

*None of you believed me when I told you, and now you'll have to reap the consequences.*

*Remember that calamity to come? Now's it here. You elected them. They will follow their path and drag you down it until all I said will come true.*

*You all thought I was crazy despite me giving you four years of my life.*

*Four. Whole. Years.*

*I've seen what they've done or, in your case, what they will do.*

*There will be war.*

*Your country will fall.*

*But you decided to sit on your throne of Western ease and comfort. It's hard to believe things will be difficult when you have the world at your fingertips and you live like kings compared to most others.*

*Endless food, endless water, all the information and entertainment you can handle at the touch of a button.*

*You spoiled, spoiled nation.*

*And don't for a second think I'm judging you. I can't judge what I once was. But then I lived it. I saw what happened so I came to warn you. I was honest and transparent and told you everything.*

*Even where I was from.*

*Yet you laughed. So many of you laughed.*

*Just a crazy old man who spent too much time squirreled away in a basement tinkering with old appliances and circuit boards.*

*Many of you called me an idiot.*

*I suppose on paper I am.*

*Hm. What paper? I have no formal education or any degrees to my name. Yet I found a way to come and warn you.*

*I tried.*

*I failed.*

*I tried again . . .*

*. . . and failed still.*

*But I did my best and, in the end, it's all any of us can do.*

*Unfortunately, I am only able to come and warn you once otherwise I would go back and try again. My hope is when I return home that maybe some of you believed me, that maybe some of you took a chance and tried to stop this thing before it happened. But it's going to take more than a mere handful of believers. It's going to take thousands of you to make a difference.*

*This note is being posted all over the Internet and a hardcopy is being left behind at the place I told you about—the place I'm leaving from. I even invited you to send me off . . . but no one showed.*

*Goodbye.*

*Hope things change.*

*Sincerely,*

*Teddy Stromholdt*

Teddy looked at the note then folded it into quarters and anchored it to the grass with a stone. He left most of the note visible so anyone who came across it would see it. He glanced up at the afternoon sky and took in the sun one last time. With a sigh, he turned and entered the cone-like machine and shut its heavy iron door. Once within, he sat in the armchair in the middle and glanced around at the controls.

He pulled the lever and the interior of the machine crackled to life with glowing electrical tubes. A couple sparks flew and the circuitry hummed.

"Here's to the future," he said. "Hope it's different than the one I left."

The machine jolted and he entered the timestream.

# The Trunk

All went to immediate darkness when the burlap bag was thrown over Doug's head. Whoever did it had his skull wrapped in there good and tight. The bag was quickly pulled taut the moment it was put on, forcing Doug's body to go backward. He fell into someone much larger than him and any effort to pull away or strike out was cut short when something solid knocked him across the back of his head.

Doug's world swam in darkness and something strong wrapped itself several times around where the burlap met his neck.

A second later, his feet were off the ground and there was the mini rush of wind as he fell a few feet and landed against something hard. A slam. Muffled voices through semi-thin walls.

He clawed at the bag but was unable to tear it. Around his neck were several layers of duct tape, sealing the bag in place.

An engine started; the walls around him and the floor vibrated. He knew exactly where he was: the trunk of a car.

"Hey! Help! Let me out!" Doug shouted. There was no answer. The car drove.

He kicked against the car's interior and pounded at it with his fists. He pressed up against what he assumed was the trunk's lid but couldn't get the thing to budge.

Screaming, he flailed about like a madman, hoping he'd break through something or at least make enough of a ruckus that whoever had kidnapped him would stop the car, come around back, and open the lid. Maybe then he'd somehow be able to make a break for it.

The car kept driving.

Minutes passed. A good twenty. Possibly thirty.

When the car finally stopped, he heard the doors open and the muffled voices of two guys as they got out. They spoke to each other but the words were unclear. They didn't even sound like harsh words, just ones firm and sure.

Doug kicked and punched against the interior.

The two guys didn't give him attention.

A violent force hit the car from the front.

The car started to move, slowly at first, then picked up speed. The guys must've put it in neutral and were pushing it.

The bumpy ground beneath the vehicle made the car hop, one rocky bump so big Doug lost his balance and banged his head against the trunk's floor. The car moved quicker when the angle changed and he was slammed back into the far outside end of the trunk. There was only a thin wall of metal and plastic between him and freedom and the damn trunk was locked shut.

The car sped and the bumps grew, tossing Doug around between what little room he had in there.

With a violent jolt, the car hit something hard and the splash afterward told him it was water.

A lake or a river or something.

He tried to think of where he might be, but there were any number of places with water in the city. Which ones had an uneven hill? Plenty of them.

The car began to right itself as it slowly sank into the water. Wherever he was, there had probably been a good drop off right by the shoreline. No subtle wade-in.

Soon, icy water began to seep its way into the trunk.

"Help!" He kicked against the trunk's lid. "Hey! There's somebody in here!"

Gravity took over and he felt the car sink further, and if he had any doubt, the more and more water coming in confirmed it.

It didn't take long for him to already be waist-deep, and even through the thickness of the burlap the stench of the dirty river was clear.

Or dirty lake.

Shivers raced through him and his muscles contracted from the water's cold.

"Help!"

He listened for any response.

Nothing.

Those two guys were probably laughing or were already well into their walk away from this place.

"What did I do to deserve this?" Doug asked. *Nothing, that's what.* No crimes. No crossing the wrong people. He'd done nothing wrong.

This was a joy crime, some kind of pleasure killing.

His heart sank.

The water was up to his shoulders. He tried to sit up as high as possible to get some more breathing room but the low roof of the trunk kept him pretty much where he was.

Shaking from the cold, he arched his head back to keep his mouth and nose above the waterline for as long as possible. New shivers ran through him when the water soaked through the burlap and caressed the back of his head.

"There's no way out of this," he whispered.

Shouting, he pressed up against the trunk's roof. The thing didn't budge.

The water was at his jawline.

And even if the trunk was somehow unlocked, the water pressure on top of it would ensure it stayed shut.

He wondered what kind of car he was in. Something classy? Or something beat up and run-down? He hoped it was something somewhere in the middle, like an old Camaro or Mustang.

The water covered his face and he pressed himself tight against the trunk's roof, thinking maybe he could grab a few extra millimeters of breathing space before being completely out of options.

The bag absorbed the water and the funk of the river—or lake—pierced his nostrils.

Mouth shut, he held his breath, the little air he had in there. He hadn't thought to take a deep breath prior to the water completely covering his head, not with his heart racing and panic setting in. Any moment now his lungs would pound and would be screaming for air.

Doug let himself sink a little in the minimal room he had.

It was quiet under the water.

His lungs convulsed as they instinctively wanted to gulp some air.

The icy water was in his bones now, too, and a fresh round of shaking made every limb jitter and jolt.

*Hold on. Don't breathe. Hold on. Don't breathe. Hold on. Don't*—On instinct, his body unable to take it anymore, he sucked in a lungful of water. His throat locked and he tried to cough it out but each lurch only brought in more water.

*Air.*

Doug shook.

He tried to expel the water in his lungs but nothing came out; a little more of the ice-cold water came in.

His arms and legs quivered; the shaking finally began to slow.

Then it started up again as panic set in full force.

Thoughts melted away.

Water in his lungs.

*Air.*

*I need air.*

Buzzing in his ears.

Darkness.

*Air.*

*Please . . . air.*

Burlap bag.

Water.

*Air. I need—*

Trunk.

Water.

Full lungs.

*Air.*

## The Text

X: Now.

J: Now?

X: Yes, now. Did I wake you?

J: Yes.

X: Good. It's time.

J: A little cliché, don't you think?

X: Our business is cliché, but it's what you signed on for.

J: Fair enough. Is this channel secure?

X: Of course. We don't take any chances.

J: Except that one time.

X: That was Bangkok. Twenty-four years ago. This is now. And speaking of now, you're up.

J: I'm prepared.

X: Review earlier transmission and reacquaint yourself with the details.

J: Reviewed before bed.

X: Review it again.

J: Fine.

X: All of this must be completed in exactly two hours and forty-one minutes.

J: Or sooner.

X: No. Precisely the timeframe stated. Not a minute over or under. All is on a clock. Don't tell me you forgot.

J: I didn't forget.

X: Are you sure? Because, if so, we abort. We can't have someone slip up on even the slightest detail.

J: This job is straight forward. Go in, do it, get out. Done.

X: All jobs are done via the formula you stated. Even life tasks.

J: Thanks, Dad.

X: Enough chatter. Pick-up is you-know-where at you-know-when.

J: You won't restate? I thought you said this is a secure channel?

X: Even secure channels must be kept vague. Compromise can happen at any time.

J: True. You and I know a little something about that.

X: Chatter. Enough. You have to leave in precisely twelve minutes to make your deadline. You best get ready. Notify me when the mission is complete.

J: I won't need to. The world will know soon after.

## Mercy

Axiom-man flew speeding past the cop cars parked outside of the house and crashed through the bay window at the front. He landed amidst a shower of glass just as the guy in front of him pulled the butcher knife from the woman's chest. The man let the body fall to the floor. The front room was spattered in blood; pools of it were all over the white carpet.

So were the bodies.

Four of them: the woman's, two young boys, and one little girl who couldn't have been older than three.

Axiom-man lunged at him; the man returned the assault.

With a quick deflection of the guy's hand, Axiom-man diverted the knife coming straight for his gut, then followed up with an energy blast from his eyes to the man's wrist, forcing him to drop it. He grabbed the guy by the shoulders and whirled him around, but not before once again catching sight of the bloody bodies on the floor. The boys—each had their throats cut. The girl—her left arm was severed from the elbow down and part of her cheek was missing.

Boiling with rage, his heart racing in adrenaline-fueled guilt for not getting here sooner, Axiom-man took the guy to the floor with a trip behind the man's leg then dove on top of him, landing on his chest. The next second, he brought his fists down on the man's head, his knuckles reveling in each impact. The man's cheekbones cracked from the blows as Axiom-man wailed on him with abandon. For the briefest of moments, the guy feebly tried to fight him off; Axiom-man shoved the guy's hands to the side. He blasted both of the man's wrists with more energy from his eye beams than was necessary then got back to work pummeling the guy's face.

The man's nose broke, as did the bone sockets around his eyes.

Shrieking, Axiom-man tore into him and felt his strength level rising to the same he'd use on Redsaw or Battle Bruiser.

The man's head lolled to the side; he no doubt fell unconscious several blows back.

Axiom-man fired up the energy beams in his eyes again and let the power build.

He'd blow this guy's head off.

Four people dead.

Three *children* dead.

Cut *into* and dead.

Blood everywhere.

The cops did nothing and let this animal kill his family. Why was it up to him to arrive on the scene to stop the killing spree? Why couldn't those who were supposed to be in charge of law and order do something?

This guy . . . this killer . . .

Axiom-man'd visit it back on him. End him like the man had ended his wife and kids.

Justice.

Balance the scales.

Growling, Axiom-man let the energy in his eyes grow and grow until all he saw was blue-white light.

He'd decimate this guy.

The man deserved it.

Deserved the pain from the punches. Deserved the energy blasts.

Deserved to die.

A small whimper came from off to the side.

Axiom-man's ears picked it up, but he thought maybe—just maybe—it was his own voice squeaking out as he considered what the man had done to these poor people. But there it was again. Small. High-pitched.

Desperate.

Axiom-man let the light fade a little from his eyes and glanced over to see the little girl stir. She looked at him, fear making her face question him as to what was going on.

He let the light fade more.

She reached toward him with trembling fingers from her remaining hand. Her eyes met his, tears around their edges, terrified.

Her arm fell and the life left her eyes.

That look.

That pain.

That fear.

Axiom-man looked back at the man.

Though she never said a word, the girl had pleaded for the terror to end.

The light of his power faded from his eyes and Axiom-man stared at the bloody mess he created beneath him. If he killed this man . . . . He couldn't do it despite wanting to. He couldn't be the one to say if this man lived or died.

But he had to stop the madness—both his own and this man's. He had to rise above the thick darkness that had descended upon this house tonight.

He had to bring justice . . . through mercy.

The guy would have to live with what he'd done, and the pain of that would have to be enough. He could very well have killed himself afterward to avoid that as so often happened in situations like these. He needed to stay alive and pay the price through a lifetime of mental torment by rotting in jail.

Axiom-man got to his feet, shaking.

He didn't think he'd ever be the same after tonight.

# Final Entry

September 8, 1897

Dear Diary,

Tonight is the night I leave.

I thought I'd be ready for this, but I was wrong. It was easy to dream and plan and hope. It's a far different thing to actually do it. The reasons are clear, to be sure, but are they enough? I've told you, Dear Diary, about the whys and the whos and the hows. You know all this.

What do you think?

I've made the necessary preparations. It took many nights while the others were asleep, but now . . . now all is in order.

The amulet is where I told you: in a clay jar behind the brick wall behind the bookcase. It was hard to chisel and remove the bricks then re-lay them while others slept and not make a sound.

The map leading to its whereabouts is also hidden in Jamie's locket. When she's old enough—she's merely two, if you remember—she'll discover it there, unfold it, and find the amulet she is destined to possess.

My time with it is over, and I've used my portion of its power.

The moment I took it off was the moment I aged four hundred years. Granted, I do not look over four hundred, but have gone from a woman of thirty-four to one of ninety. That's four lifetimes, including this one. Three other families, with a total of four husbands and fourteen children.

My daughter has the same fate.

And the same pain.

Should she not find the map, eventually the amulet will call to her and will draw her toward it. Its pull will be so strong she will not be able to resist it lest she fear her own death from not possessing it. Sadly, death is what will happen should she not put it on. She's marked for it. Not by her own doing or intentionally by me. It's what she's inherited through blood—the last female heir must take hold of it once their mother uses her part of its power.

And O what power she will have.

She will command winds and stir up oceans. The trees will bow before her and mighty walls will crumble from a mere glance. Men will strive to possess her and will stumble over their feet just to be by her side. She will have the favor of children and people everywhere.

Jamie could rule the world, if she so chose. But that is also a test from the amulet: the usage of its power, for its use will determine the length of that use.

Sadly, I fear, the amulet has grown weary from generations of improper stewardship. Some have indeed used it to brighten the world. Others have used it to darken it, and, so far as I understand, it has been used for darkness far more than for light, and darkness takes a greater toll on its power stores.

I hope my daughter chooses wisely.

I hope she brings light and life.

It's all I can wish.

Now, I must say goodbye without warning, for who can explain to a darling husband how a loving wife and the star of his eye suddenly turned into an old woman? Especially to a man who doesn't believe in magic. I know my Robert. Even a final demonstration of what the amulet enabled me to do would have been met with skepticism and some scramble to find a scientific reason behind it. And now, with the amulet removed from me, it forbids me from putting it back on because my time with it is over.

The children: Timothy, David, and Jamie.

The boys are older. David is fifteen and quite cerebral so will be able to process my disappearance well. Jamie will forget me quickly. Timothy is twelve and has always been by my side. He will have the hardest time. I hope Robert will be able to comfort him.

This is my final entry, Dear Diary. I will bring you with me and prior to my passing from this world mail you to my Jamie with instructions for you not to be opened until she has reached her thirteenth year. She will find within your pages understanding as to why I left and guidance as to how to use the amulet for good.

I will miss you, Dear Diary. You have always been my confidante, and thanks to the amulet, have even spoken to me.

Goodbye, Dear Diary.

Goodbye, my family.

I love you.

Goodbye.

- Rosemary

## Tub Words

Fourteen books.

The first four were duds. It was *Death Trap 9000* that did it and skyrocketed Ray Fortier to stardom. Every book written after that was an automatic hit even if sometimes the books themselves were so-so.

Name power was everything.

And those first four duds? Those got a nice boost once *Death Trap 9000* captivated sci-fi audiences everywhere and launched a series of sequels and side adventures. The star of the series wasn't an alien, nor some lone tough-guy captain who traversed planet to planet, scored alien babes, and stopped intergalactic wars. It was the ship, a tiny one-man vessel called the *Star Arrow* that resonated with readers. It was fully-armed, could cloak, and was nigh invincible. It traveled through space and also functioned as an all-terrain vehicle when zipping around a planet's surface or exploring its oceans or sailing through its skies.

But that was in the books. Here on Planet Earth, the *Star Arrow* was Ray's bathtub. He didn't write at a desk. Couldn't. It was those first four flops that were written while sitting at a wooden desk in his den, him punching one key after another on his laptop. Writing those first four books had been *work*. A lot of work. It was hard to get the flow going and get in the zone. But one day while soaking in the tub, the *Death Trap* idea came and he couldn't help but get going on it right away. Instead of getting out and drying off, dressing then writing, he hopped out of the tub, grabbed his laptop, then got back into the water and sat with his knees up, laptop balanced on them, and began to type. The story flowed like beer from a barrel. The passage of time vanished and it was only when the water got cold did he realize he'd been at it for a couple of hours already.

Later, once out of the tub and dried off, Ray read what he'd written and couldn't believe the same guy who wrote four crappy books had written something so exciting. He tried picking up the story sitting at his desk and each tap at the keyboard was like plunking a finger down on heavy, sticking piano keys. Curiosity getting the better of him, he brought the laptop to the tub and, sure enough—settled and comfortable in the hot water—the tub around him became the *Star Arrow* and the story poured out. The rest, as they say, was history.

Every installment since was tub-written. In the tub, Ray lived the adventures as first-hand as he could.

Today, the water was hot; the laptop was hot, too, and the story sizzled. He was almost done.

He adjusted the computer on his lap and flipped the cord onto the other side of the shampoo bottle on the tub's rim. He learned about eight books back the battery on this thing had a short life—a few hours—so keeping the thing plugged in was the only way to get things done.

Ray wrote.

The *Star Arrow* had just delivered a bomb to Arantes's core, the planet's center functioning as a power source for the whole place. Arantes had been taken over by the Hlox and the planet had been overrun. Some of Arantes's residents had escaped—enough of them to repopulate their race elsewhere—but if the Hlox got off-planet, they'd do the same to another world.

They had to be destroyed.

The bomb was in place and the *Star Arrow* raced out of the long tunnel from the core to get out of harm's way.

Ray leaned forward and the laptop rocked. He caught it just in time before it tipped over into the water.

The ship still had several thousand miles to go but the *Star Arrow*'s engines would get to the surface in no time.

Ray had an idea: The bomb would prematurely go off. He set the narrative in motion. The core erupted. The explosion sent earthquakes throughout the planet. Fire engulfed the *Star Arrow*'s path.

"Go, go, go," Ray said.

The ship had to hurry.

Another earthquake.

Ray rocked in the tub from the impact.

The laptop rocked, too.

Tipped.

He caught it. Set it on his lap.

The *Star Arrow* burst through the hole in the ground and headed straight for the sky. In a few seconds, it'd be at the atmosphere. Fire rapidly swarmed over the planet. The Hlox shrieked and squealed as they burned.

Almost there. Almost out.

The *Star Arrow* broke the atmosphere and flew into space.

The planet blew up.

Yes!

Ray shot his hands into the air. Victory.

The laptop hit the water.

In seconds, a violent shock ripped through the tub and penetrated Ray's bones and muscles. He couldn't move and fell over, his face going under its depth. Convulsing and shaking, he rode the shockwave of the Arantes explosion.

As his heart cut out, at least he knew the Hlox were destroyed.

## Broken

Sometimes things fall apart and absolutely crumble.

Peter sat in the easy chair and simply stared at his knees. He couldn't believe things had gotten this bad. How did he arrive here? What happened? Well, he knew *what* happened, but what had been in motion to get him here?

Everything was gone.

His family, his job, any hope for the future.

There were dreams—and they all came crashing down.

There was no one he could call right now, anyone to just listen so he could unload the whirlwind inside of him.

His heart was laced with sharp pain. The medication his doctor prescribed to help take the edge off the depression and anxiety wasn't working.

Peter just sat there.

Shocked.

Broken.

A gun on the table beside him.

He didn't know if he would make it.

## Odd Hunting

Grug lumbered over to the silver tub sitting there in the forest. It was open, some rainwater from the shower just moments ago having gathered within. There was a lid, which he rocked back and forth a little on its hinges. The dark gray clouds above signaled more rain was on its way. He went around the tub, surveying all sides, seeing what else was near it—nothing other than some grass and fallen leaves. But inside . . . inside was a hunk of raw meat. Dinner.

Thunder crashed overhead and almost immediately it began to downpour. Grug got into the tub for shelter and pulled the lid closed. Its top was transparent and so he watched as the water splashed against it in a blurry mosaic, showcasing some of the skeletal trees while he ate the meat.

A red light flashed within the tub and a voice said: *Initiating temporal sequence.* Immediately after, a purple mist sprayed from tiny nozzles along each side of the tub. It tasted like earthworm mixed with pine. Grug's head swam and all went dark.

He didn't know how much time had passed—maybe a few seconds, perhaps a few minutes—but when he came to, men covered in connected tiny ringlets of dark gray— stone?—with strange pointed head coverings clunked against the tub with thick sticks with triangular ends.

"Oy, look at this," one of the men said. "There's someone inside."

The other guy came up close and peered in. "You in there. Open up."

Grug banged against the transparent covering with all his might but couldn't break through. One of the men on the outside smashed against it with that tool of his.

A fresh blast of purple mist filled the tub and Grug went back under.

When he awoke, he saw a couple of men in white frilly shirts hitting the outside of the tub with long carved sticks made of wood and . . . stone again? It didn't look like stone but he didn't know the word for the long dark gray cylinders coming out of the end of them.

Through the barrier, one said, "Hey, you in there? Open this thing."

"Look at him, all hairy and matted. What is he?" said the other man.

More banging against the tub's hull.

Grug banged against the interior of it with his fists and feet, but he couldn't get out.

A fresh blast of purple mist put him back under.

Grug wasn't sure how much time had passed until he awoke again, this time to three men wearing brown hide from head to toe. They beat on the tub with sticks that had stones crisscrossed with hide, holding the two together.

"Open," one said. "Open."

Grug grunted his reply, once more kicking and pounding against the inside of the tub. The thuds from the men's tools echoed within the narrow chamber, each beat of the tools matching the hard thumping of his heart.

One of the men on the outside raised his tool good and high above the transparent roof and Grug was sure it would break through. The thing came crashing down and bounced off.

Frustrated and growling, Grug threw himself around inside the chamber, banging himself against all sides in a furious effort to get out. Nothing changed.

Trapped. Utterly trapped.

Another blast of purple mist, and the next time he awoke a handful of young men wearing shirts of various colors cut off at the sleeves along with blue pants jumped up and down on top of the tub. Some kicked at it from the outside. Others threw heavy stones at it. Each slam of the stones against the tub made Grug cringe from the off chance one would smash through and hit him.

"Look at this guy," one of the younger men said. "He looks like Chewbacca."

Another of the young men laughed. "No kidding. What is he?"

"Looks like a caveman to me," another said.

Grug hit against the tub's interior again, but his efforts were cut short by more mist. All went black. An indeterminate amount of time passed.

When he came to, an older man with gray hair and tidy gray clothes was on the other side of the transparent lid. The man leaned in close and did something with his hand outside of Grug's view. A loud hiss followed and the lid opened.

"Easy, friend," the man said, extending a hand to him.

Grug didn't take it and instead lunged out and tackled the man to the ground. Immediately, harsh vibrations raced through every bone and muscle in his body and everything locked up. He was hauled off the man by two other men and brought to his feet. The man in gray got off the ground, dusted himself off, then stepped up to Grug.

The man said, "You've been through quite a journey." The man stepped aside and with an open hand showed what was behind him: a multitude of tall structures with tubs similar to what Grug had just been in traveling this way and that through the air. "Welcome to the year 2142. It's time for you to join the others." Then, with a grin, "After all, winter is coming and we don't want to go hungry and there's nothing quite like prehistoric steak."

# The Suit

It was a disgusting thing, the suit.

All of it. Every stitch, every clasp.

Darwin wished it inspired hope. Instead, it inspired despair . . . and pain. The suit—never hope. That wasn't the point of it. It was a reminder of what happened. The red slash marks that served as the uniform's symbol mimicked the same slash marks that tore open his wife's body, leaving her lungs and entrails on the sidewalk. The red marks along the right leg that at a casual glance might look like lightning bolts were the gashes that tore open her thigh when the man came at her with a knife.

This suit, this thing of hatred and unforgiveness. This thing of beauty and anarchy and freedom.

This damned black suit that mirrored a darkened soul.

Nothing but red and black.

Nothing but blood and darkness.

He hated it. Cursed it. Despised it.

But he needed it.

It was *him*.

It was his wife.

It was her bloody body he saw fall to the concrete like a torn-open ragdoll, and it was him just standing there crippled in fear because some joker had a knife that was probably no more than five inches long. But that knife was sharp. It cut into her and split her open like she was nothing. But she wasn't nothing. She was his wife.

His love.

His life.

And the man got away. He'd wanted nothing. No money. No jewels. Not anything other than to just show up and gut a woman while the man who was supposed to be her hero looked on in paralyzing fear.

Darwin the coward.

Darwin tried killing himself after that. Couldn't live with the guilt. But each time he tried, all he saw in his mind's eye was this bloody suit—black and terrible, red and dripping with his wife's life force. Was it her? Was it a message from the great beyond telling him what to do or what to become or who he really was or her sharing her pain?

This suit. It stood before him now in its chamber.

The night she died was ten years ago.

The night Darwin the coward died was nine.

Black and red.

Blood and darkness.

Night Blade.

# Beneath

My wife Moira and I have no idea if this transmission will reach the surface. From what we understand, communication with the aboveground has been met with silence.

We hope you weren't overtaken by the Runners, those mutant bastards who drove us all down beneath the earth's surface to begin with.

I'm sending this via the radio setup put in place when we originally got down here eight years ago. No one has come and gone since, but those of us beneath and those of you above, we all know of each other.

Moira's pregnant.

A dumb move on my part, I know. We didn't take precaution and now we have a little life on the way in just under eight months. Call it ensuring survival of the species but, as said, there wasn't active "ensurance" of survival on my part. Things happen. But, in the end, I guess it doesn't matter. These caves won't hold up much longer. The structural supports keeping the roof up were put together in haste and by engineers still learning their trade.

The walls have begun to crumble around us. I can't even remember how far down we are anymore. A thousand feet? Two thousand? More?

In the end, I fear, we're all going to be dead. Most of the exit ways that were once bright hallways of hope for when the war above was over have collapsed. Some men are working to try and dig a way out. They could be at it past a lifetime depending on how much there is.

As for Moira and I, we're holed up in the transmission room with the walls shaking and a few paltry food items that might—*might*—see us through the next few days. A week at the most.

The door to this room got blocked by a huge hunk of rock that fell just on the other side of the door. I've been working on prying at the hinges with a measly wrench but it's slow-going and I'm barely doing more than scratching the framing.

At least it gives Moira hope. It makes her believe there's a chance—however slim—for our unborn child.

Personally, I think she's lost all concept of time and doesn't understand we don't have what we need in here for the remaining months of gestation never mind the remaining days until this whole place falls on us and kills us.

I want to personally thank you up there for your service. No matter what's happening with the war, I'm sure you've held out as long as you could. I've seen firsthand what those venom sprays from their mouths do to people so I salute you from the depths of my heart for fighting for us.

Hang on . . .

A wall's crumbling beside me.

Where's Moira?
Moira!
Oh no . . . her face . . . her . . . her head.
Moira!

## Dave's Bar

There was something about Dave's Bar that Ignatius found charming.

It wasn't the company. He'd known enough brawlers and guys down on their luck over the years. It wasn't the girls in high-cut skirts with a bit of cleavage showing that did it for him either. Not that he didn't appreciate it, but as part of the Order of Friars Minor, his eyes weren't supposed to deviate to that stuff anyway. It wasn't even the mug of beer he was drinking. The secret tavern room at the order had enough of that.

It was the otherworldliness of Dave's that got to him. It was a place removed from all he knew, a place to just sit by himself and mull over the week, sometimes the years. Sure, he got looks and the odd comment sent his way—it wasn't every day you saw a priest in a bar. Even some said—what with his brown robe and all—he looked like a Jedi. But that's as far as it went. Even the worst and bottom level of humanity still had the fear of God running through them and to mess with a holy man was like mucking with God Himself.

A fight broke out behind him. He glanced over his shoulder, but as a pacifist didn't get involved and just took another swig of beer.

When he was done his drink, he let out a small burp then scanned the bar for Dave. Dave seldom worked the bar himself. Instead, he preferred the sanctity of the back room and liked to run things from there.

Particularly, Dave and Ignatius had a special arrangement: Ignatius could come in for a beer as long as he didn't cause any trouble, and he knew the kind of trouble Dave was referring to and it had nothing to do with preaching.

"Thank you," Ignatius said to Delores, who worked the bar.

She nodded in his direction then turned her attention to another customer. She then glanced his way again and nodded toward the backroom. Ignatius grinned his understanding then got up from his stool and side-stepped the fight. That poor soul. He should have dodged to the left then delivered a right punch straight to the other guy's mouth.

Ignatius went to the backroom and knocked three times, paused, then knocked twice.

The door opened.

Ignatius went in.

Dave was alone and in the room's corner shadows despite the eight-foot-square fireplace going strong in the middle.

"Enjoy yourself?" Dave asked.

"Yes, thank you. Bless you," Ignatius replied.

Ignatius stood before the fire.

"Will see you again," Dave said. It wasn't a question.

Ignatius simply nodded, and when the flame turned green and swirled with black smoke, he stepped into the fire. It washed its green glow around him and he emerged in the backroom of his order.

1249 AD.

# The Shot

2016 had been one hell of a year.

Declan had lost his family to a car wreck. He'd been the driver.

He'd lost his wife, his son, his daughter, and newborn baby.

It was New Year's Eve.

Declan put the gun to the side of his head and blew his brains out.

## The Drive

Janna was reluctant to head back into her old neighborhood. It was fairly glamorous compared to the rest of the city—big houses, fancy front doors, bay windows. Every garage was at least a double. Some a triple.

But, she knew its secrets . . . and Mike lived out here.

Mike. Tall, handsome, charming. The kind of guy any woman would fall head over heels for.

But she knew this area. She knew the houses were just facades for things better left unknown. Like the Johnson residence. Jim Johnson liked to beat his wife. Sometimes his kids. She drove past the house and noticed the curtains covering the windows.

A little further down the street and she came up to the Bagleys. Mrs. Bagley—she didn't know her first name—liked to hit the bottle hard, which sometimes led to her hitting the walls and any piece of furniture she could find, especially the expensive china in the cabinet in the dining room. Janna knew this after walking past there one night in her teens and overhearing the cops out front who were called to the scene.

She kept going. Christmas lights twinkled in some of the windows and shone bright around garage doors. During her childhood, Christmas out here was magical despite the Scrooges that lived inside most places.

Too bad Mike had to make his home on her old stomping ground.

Stomping. All those walks to school trudging through a foot of snow. All the times she had to climb the stairs up to her bedroom at her parents' command because the neighbors were getting loud.

On the left were the Defrens. Model parents and strong Christians. It was their kids that had been wayward and on more than one occasion got caught dealing pot. The youngest, Kyle, also threatened his brother with a kitchen knife.

Janna's parents had moved out a long time ago. They got a condo closer to the city, and also closer to her place.

But tonight, she needed to see Mike. *Had* to see him. It was that beautiful smile of his that made him so inviting, but she put that out of her mind. She couldn't think about that right now. The thought of the homes she passed were too intrusive.

On the right was old Granny Fairchild. Janna wasn't sure if the ancient woman was still alive but rumor had it the place was haunted. Granny would often tell the kids stories of objects being moved in the middle of the night, like that one time she found the toaster on her sofa instead of in the kitchen where it belonged.

Mike's place was coming up.

Janna's heart picked up a beat and she parked on the road a few houses down.

She turned the car off and eyed the place. The front room light was on and she'd caught word from her informant Mike would be home tonight.

She reached into her purse and pulled out the gun and verified the silencer was in place.

This would be an easy hit.

# The Writer

*Retreat*, Warren King thought. *You can't do this. You can't handle it.*

Warren eyed the computer in front of him, the silver glow of its screen the only light in the dark and dank room.

He knew as a bestselling novelist the first line was everything. It was the hook that got the reader to read the rest of the book.

*"The gray wolf entered the room."*

*No, not good enough*, he thought.

*"The silvery gray wolf snuck in unannounced, its very presence putting a strange-yet-terrifying warmth on the air."*

*Better*, Warren thought, *but not good enough. Come on. Be a man. Face it down.*

*"All it took was for the silver-gray wolf to make its presence known and Tim fell to his knees before it."*

*You're getting there*, Warren thought. He slowly paced in front of the silver glow, sweat dripping down his face, his heart beating fast. *Come on. It has to be perfect. This could be your last story. The final one. Make it good. Open strong, end even stronger.* Though he had his doubts about that last part. The stress of crafting the perfect narrative for his swansong might do him in once and for all.

He took a step toward the screen, his legs suddenly drained of their strength. He collapsed before the monitor and barely managed to squeeze out some words.

*"The gray wolf's fur glistened in the minimal moonlight, its cold, dead white eyes revealing nothing but death."*

*I could live with that one,* Warren thought. *Might have no other choice.* He inhaled deep then exhaled everything, doing what he could to calm himself.

A final story.

A final effort.

Aimed-at perfection for his literary legacy.

The silver screen shone brighter, as if the monitor moved closer on its own accord.

Warren's heart swam up into his neck, its pulse thumping there and still somehow in his chest. His skin was slick with sweat, all over now, even on his legs. His mouth went dry.

*"The wolf came in like a shadow, blending into the darkness. It was only when the stars shone their light into the den's opening and revealing its fur did Tim realize he wasn't alone."*

Warren Timothy King's head swam and the walls of his writing room crumbled and turned into the rocky interior of the den. The monitor before him morphed into the silver wolf, its white eyes seeing into him, its high sense of smell no doubt picking up the scent of panicking blood swimming through his veins.

*"The wolf drew closer."*

*That's the one,* Warren thought. *Simple and direct.* And, he knew, by the hungry gaze in the wolf's eyes, there would be no middle chapters.

He skipped to the last page.

*"The wolf pounced on Tim, and the last thing he smelled and tasted was his own blood while his internal organs were ripped open by crimson-stained teeth."*

# The Crash

The Toyota Camry went airborne at one hundred and three kilometers an hour the moment it hit the slick patch of ice on the road. The hydro pole filled the windshield and a million shiny stars filled Carl's vision as the glass shattered and its pieces sped toward him. A thousand cuts and stings ripped across his face and hands, and although they all happened nearly simultaneously, he could pick out each one and felt the warm blood trickle from each slash.

The steering wheel came at him at lightning speed and his face smashed against it, teeth bursting forth from their resting place in his gums. Blood filled his mouth. The leather covering at the top of the wheel slammed into his eyes and when his head flew back after the impact, his neck cracked and he went momentarily blind and envisioned his eyeballs left stuck to the steering wheel.

Darkness.

Then light.

Then the hydro pole up close and personal, the Camry folded against it in a tight U.

Carl's head throbbed, and there was immense pressure against his forehead even though he was leaning back in his seat, his head touching nothing. He tried to reach up to see if his head had caved in from hitting the wheel but couldn't move his arm. It was pinned between the right side of the chair and the deep indent from the pole. He tried his left hand and found it had somehow gotten behind his body in a chicken wing-like angle. Realizing this sent his shoulder ablaze with pain, his left hand and fingers numb.

The front of the car was folded inward and on top of him, keeping his legs from moving.

Cell phone.

He had a cell phone.

Front left pocket.

But how to dial without fingers?

He tried nodding his head forward in an effort to grab it with his remaining teeth. Where he'd go from there or how he would dial, he didn't know. It didn't matter anyway. The deep and pounding pain at the base of his neck gave him a splitting headache that forbade any movement to retrieve the phone.

The cuts sang their glorious sting, especially on his right cheek. He could only imagine a concentration of torn-open flesh. Blood dripped from his jaw.

Warm blood seeped from his mouth and the agony of what had to have been at least six teeth forcefully extracted sent his gums into a rollercoaster of shockwave after shockwave of pain.

He closed his swollen eyes. Even that was excruciating the moment the skin of his eyelids touched each other.

His breathing came in shallow gasps and he wondered if his lungs had somehow been punctured. With what or to what extent, he didn't know. He tried to calm himself, take slow breaths, focus on his ears. Aside from the sting of the cuts along their skin, they seemed to be all right.

He listened for any oncoming cars.

The road was quiet.

Head pounding, he tried to surface thoughts of his wife and wondered if at that moment she knew he was in trouble even though she was twenty-some-odd kilometers away. They were newly-weds. Did she sense him somehow? Did she know something was wrong?

All faded to black.

Carl awoke again. Could've been five minutes later, could've been an hour. It was impossible to tell.

That hydro pole still loomed over him as if in victory.

The outside cold poured in from the open windshield and he trembled from the chill. When he had left the house, it was minus twenty-seven degrees, but with the wind chill it was probably somewhere around minus thirty-five.

The warmth of his blood had cooled. It wasn't even damp anymore. He opened and closed his mouth, the frozen blood cracking with each pull.

Air barely came into his lungs. Something had got him. He focused and searched his peripheral vision for an indicator of what the issue might be. At the bottom of his vision a black bar stuck out of his chest. It took him a moment to realize it was the windshield wiper. Whether it was the wiper itself or the handle that controlled it, he couldn't tell from this angle. Regardless, it had him, and with his body starting to lock up, he could barely take in another sip of air.

He listened once more for sounds on the road.

All was quiet.

All went dark.

When he came to again, someone yelled at him. The voice seemed far off, though out of the corner of his eye he saw a guy in a dark paramedic's uniform leaning into the vehicle.

"You okay?" the man asked. "Hey, buddy, wake up. You okay? Can you hear me?"

Carl tried to nod but couldn't move. He noticed another man had appeared beside the paramedic. This one wore a robe of sparkling white; the fabric glowed so bright and shone like the sun Carl had to close his eyes.

He didn't know which man would reach out to him first.

## Humanity

It was Tuesday and Martin was at the mall people watching, something he unexpectedly found himself enjoying while one day waiting on his wife while she tried on pants in another store.

He sat on the bench in the main aisle between the shops, legs crossed, eyes on his lap. With his eyesight recently giving him a hard time, he put the focus on his ears and listened to humanity.

\* \* \*

"She said it was around here somewhere . . ." a man said, voice trailing.

\* \* \*

"Eighty-four bucks and change. Not a deal at all," said another guy, this one sounding young.

\* \* \*

A child giggling.

\* \* \*

Muddled voices for a few moments, then—

"I have cancer," a guy said, "the kind you don't get better from."

\* \* \*

"Really?" she exclaimed. "That's great! When did you guys mee—No, not him. Come on! He's fugly as hell. You're crazy."

\* \* \*

"Moooommm."

"I said no. We have to go pick up Dad from work and we're already late."

\* \* \*

"Don't think we'll make the mortgage this week. Just found out EI's ran out. Sorry, babe."

\* \* \*

Glass shattered a few stores down on the right. Someone said something but Martin couldn't make out what.

More voices all melded together as one.

\* \* \*

A girl: "The guy's a dork."

"So are you," another girl said.

\* \* \*

"So, so late. Dammit!"

\* \* \*

"I thought the food court was—"

\* \* \*

The guy's voice was like steel: "Tell him one-thirty-five firm or we're not getting it."

\* \* \*

"Oh Lord, watch over them," she said.

\* \* \*

Sudden silence. No one walked by.
Minutes passed.

\* \* \*

"Do you think you can move any slower?" she said.
"Ow. You're hurting my arm!" the little boy said.
"Come on!"

\* \* \*

"Those cards go in this rack."

\* \* \*

The wet sound of a kiss.

\* \* \*

Martin looked up.
People walked by.
Martin looked down . . . and listened again.

## Rescue Bot

The burst of static before TW1047's eyes cleared, revealing the car wreck before it—two vehicles completely intertwined, one an SUV, the other a semi.

People within.

*Accessing Time Lapse Function.*

Scanning the way the front of the semi sat partially on top of the SUV while the sides of the massive truck hugged the other vehicle, TW1047 activated its Time Lapse Function and watched the collision as if it happened anew.

The semi drove at one hundred and three kilometers an hour. It headed straight to where TW1047 stood. The SUV quickly veered in from the right, taking over the semi's lane. The two vehicles became no more than thirty-seven feet apart. There would have been a brief moment for the SUV to correct its course, but instead the two vehicles collided. The semi drove on top and through the SUV, metal intertwining with metal. The vehicles ground to a halt, and the Time Lapse was over.

Another burst of static spread across TW1047's vision. Something wasn't right. Static spreads were not common.

*Accessing Priority Rescue Assessment.*

*Three lifeforms located. One critical. Two others critical. Former easiest to assist.*

TW1047's robot legs kicked into gear and it stomped toward the driver side of the semi. Once in place, it reached out its mechanical arms and drove its pincer-like hands into the door. With a twist of its wrists, it locked the pincers in and took a firmer grip of the metal. With a pull, it jerked away the door, revealing the driver within. The driver was a heavyset male slumped in his seat. The front dash was pressed all the way up against him. Blood oozed out along where the man and semi were connected.

TW1047 took another scan but not before a spurt of black and white static ran across its vision.

*Reporting Error Code 2814.* The robot sent out the signal to Fox-tech, alerting its creators to the static malfunction.

Using its built-in X-ray, TW1047 detected multiple breaks in the man's legs and several torn and compressed muscles.

*Running Rescue Scenario A4.*

A moment later, TW1047's programming told it it was safe to pull the man out. Putting one pincer against the dash and the other in between the man's legs against the seat, TW1047 pried the two apart, freeing the driver. TW1047 brought its arms in close and used one pincer to snip the driver's seat belt. Getting its metal arms under the driver, TW1047 carefully pulled the man's body from the wreckage then turned and walked toward the waiting paramedics.

Another burst of static, this one longer. It was quickly followed by a second burst as TW1047 lay the man's body on a gurney.

*Repeat reporting Error Code 2814.*

Turning back to the collision, TW1047 headed toward the SUV. Once at the SUV's doors, another static blink scattered across its vision. The robot inserted its pincers into the passenger side's door and locked them in place. With a pull, TW1047 removed the door, revealing the woman and child within.

Static tore across TW1047's vision again.

*System override.*

White-on-black coding filled the robot's sight.

*Program download complete. Execute.*

TW1047 took note of the look of relief upon the woman's cut-up face. She was compressed against the dash with the steering wheel pressed up and under her ribs.

"My son . . . my son. Get my son," she said.

TW1047 turned to see a terrified little boy covered in shattered glass and stuck between the rear seat and the passenger's. The boy's eyes were closed.

*Combatting system virus.*

A static burst. *System override. Execute.*

*Running virus protection.*

Another static burst. *System override. Execute.*

*Deleting new download.*

Static filled TW1047's vision. *Program download complete. Execute.*

When its vision cleared, it read: *Virus removal program fail.*

Static. Numbers. White-on-black. *System override. Execute.*

The robot reached in and extended its pincers to the boy and the woman and clamped them around their necks . . . and began to squeeze.

## Blood Angel

Joey St. Claire—*the* Joey St. Claire—let the blood flow freely from the vertical slits in his wrists as he sat against the bathroom wall. The lightbulb flickered; the blood-stained razorblade sat on the tiled floor beside him.

The warmth of hot blood ran down his palms, tickled his fingers.

Thirty-six million albums sold; he had all the money in the world. But it didn't matter, didn't alleviate the pain inside. People cheered for him, girls threw themselves at him. The stage was his.

Thrills, adrenaline, worship.

On stage he was alive . . . but only on the outside. Inside, he burned and cried. He never got over losing his mom to a house fire when he was eight; never got over his uncle beating him just because he couldn't have a son of his own. Never got over true love and having his heart destroyed four times over.

Never got over the fact no one seemed to recognize the hero on stage was just a lonely young adult crying out, his music and lyrics a display of a broken heart.

Blood pooled around him. Joey closed his eyes and waited for his forever sleep to come.

A bright light shining through his eyelids jolted him out of his stupor. A man with lightning for eyes and giant white wings dripping with sparkling crimson blood stood before him. The blood dissolved into nothing just before it hit the floor.

"Joey," he said. His voice was calm but carried an undertone of thunder.

Half-asleep from the blood loss, Joey could merely acknowledge this otherworldly being's presence. If he had the energy, his heart would no doubt be galloping and he'd bolt from the room.

Joey studied the man's shining armor: silver splashed with blood, and a belt made of gold with a longsword hanging from a sheath.

"Joey," the man said again.

*I'm Joey*, he thought.

The man held out his hand and Joey felt compelled to take it with trembling fingers. He did, and this man—this "blood angel"—pulled him to his feet.

"Come with me," the blood angel said.

He put his arm around Joey and held him tight. Soon, the giant crimson-splashed wings spread out and their feet left the floor. They flew through the roof as if it wasn't there and, just before they left the bathroom, Joey took note of his body still leaning against the bathroom wall, blood growing in a circle around it.

"I'm dead," Joey said.

"Not dead. Just removed."

They flew past the roof of the vintage building and entered the night sky. Quickly, they picked up speed and the city below rushed by in a blur.

The blood angel still holding him firm, Joey was taken to a rundown house in the suburbs. The two floated down through the roof and were in a living room with a tipped-over couch and knocked-over lamp. Joey noticed the man and the woman in the room cast long shadows on the wall but he and the blood angel didn't.

The woman beat on the man, punching him in the face and kicking him in the groin. It was clear the man restrained himself from retaliating.

"I hate you, I hate you, I hate you!" she screamed. Then, softly with tears, "I love you."

The man's face went soft and he said, "I love you, too."

The blood angel swept Joey up and took him back through the roof. They were in the night sky again, the city once more a blur beneath them.

They went to another house and entered through the walls into a kitchen.

"Don't believe me the stove is hot?" the woman said. The bright red glow from the hot element cast her in demonic crimson light.

"I do. I promise," the boy said. He looked no more than five.

"I'll show you," she said and jerked the boy's hand toward the hot element.

He resisted and she slapped him. In his daze, she took his hand and placed it on the burner. His screams drowned out the sizzle of burning flesh.

Joey and the blood angel were suddenly in the sky again. The world turned into a rushing mosaic and Joey found himself in another room, this one with walls made of what appeared to be clay.

A man stood before another man who was on his knees, a gun pointed at the kneeling man's head.

"Please, I beg you, spare me," the man on his knees said.

The gun went off; blood and brain spattered the wall behind him.

Back in the air, another rush of the world.

Then all cleared and, on the ground, a school bus filled with children singing turned a corner. A second later a bomb went off within and their singing turned to screams as the bus ground to a halt. What looked like ISIS raiders streamed out of the surrounding alleyways and swarmed the bus. They entered and gun shots lit up the bus's interior in a series of flashes.

"No more," Joey said.

The blood angel remained silent.

They were in the air then suddenly in a hotel hallway where a young Asian girl was escorted into a room by two men twice her size. Somehow he got a sudden view of her little terrified face, tears welling in her eyes but not spilling out.

Joey's head swam and flashes of machine guns going off filled his vision. Bodies riddled with bullets and bursting open with red holes came next. Dizziness took over and he doubled forward. The blood angel straightened him and Joey had a vision: a little child, who looked like a skeleton draped in black skin, lay in the street. A vision of another child similar to the first took over and Joey heard the boy's stomach growl with hunger as if the sound came through an amplifier.

White skin dripping with blood came next, followed by a strung-out woman hurled to the floor of a dingy bathroom where she proceeded to crawl to the toilet and throw up.

"Please. Stop," Joey said.

The angel's wings flapped but not before sprinkling Joey in blood, the splash from each drop sending an electric tingle through him.

The world went ablur. A familiar rooftop appeared beneath his feet. A descent. A bathroom—Joey's body slumped over on the floor.

With a sharp gasp, Joey awoke back in his body, the blood angel in front of him.

"Do you understand?" the angel asked.

Joey looked at his wrists. They were smeared red but the wounds were closed. He coughed then threw up. After wiping his mouth, he said, "Yeah. You wanted to show me how many have it worse than me."

The angel shook his head. "Then you do not understand." His lightning eyes grew soft despite their power. "It was simply to reveal that others hurt, too. Your pain is no more and no less than theirs. They hurt. You hurt. The world hurts. Pain is pain. Earth is a fallen place. You just needed to know you are not alone. You are never alone."

The blood angel withdrew his sword and raised it high and readied it as if to stab him.

"Are you going to kill me?" Joey asked.

The blood angel didn't say a word and in one fluid motion drove the sword into Joey's heart.

Instead of pain, energy and strength filled him and flickering white lightning filled his vision. He found himself on his feet and, though his heartache abated some, it was still there. The sword was in his hand . . . then faded away.

The angel was gone but the words, "You are not alone," echoed in Joey's ears.

## Last Flight

Axiom-man found the boy's body next to the railroad track while doing a sweep of the city's perimeter. It was fortunate he'd flown low enough to see him.

He landed beside the boy and knelt down. Off in the distance, the train continued on its way and he knew there wasn't enough time to alert the engineer of what obviously happened. The boy was covered in blood on his left side, orange T-shirt and blue jeans torn from the wounds. The child's chest rose and fell in shallow breaths. It was a miracle he was still alive. The train must have just clipped him. Did the engineer even know?

Axiom-man briefly thought back to the night he first got his powers and how he discovered his ultra strength on a box car hauling telephone poles.

The boy gasped.

Axiom-man scanned his body. The kid's leg was broken, a shard of bone sticking out just below the knee. There seemed to be another break higher up on the leg but it was difficult to detect the precise damage through the mash of bloody flesh and jeans. The poor boy's arm was also broken; it looked like he had a second elbow across his bicep.

"I'm going to get you out of here," Axiom-man said gently.

The boy managed to open his eyes and a small smile rose on his lips. "Ax . . . Axiom . . ."

"I got you." Carefully—oh so carefully—Axiom-man scooped his arms under the boy. He stood, the boy in his arms, and held him close. The child winced, then his head lolled back, eyes closed.

"Hey, stay with me," Axiom-man said. He rose into the sky and immediately headed in the direction of the nearest hospital.

He kicked on the speed and flew full force. The boy howled in pain as the wind forced his little body against him. Axiom-man slowed down a little and the boy's wailing ceased. The child's eyes remained closed.

"Hey, kid, wake up," Axiom-man said. "You got to stay awake, okay?"

The boy's eyes opened a little.

*Must keep him conscious*, Axiom-man thought. *Get him talking.* "What's your name?"

The boy pursed his lips then opened his mouth to speak. "C-Colton."

"Hi, Colton. How old are you?"

"S-six" —he coughed— "and . . . th-three . . . quarters."

"You're a big boy," Axiom-man said, "and strong, too. What's your favorite color?"

"B-bl . . . blue." Colton let out a cry.

Axiom-man wondered if he was still flying too fast, but he had to keep up the speed if he was to get Colton to the hospital in time.

"My . . . l-leg," Colton said.

Axiom-man glanced down at the break again. The boy's thigh was twisted and blood started to gush from the wound.

"C-cold," Colton said.

*The break might've cut the femoral artery*, Axiom-man thought. *Must hurry.* "You'll be warm soon. Just hang on." He thought about wrapping the boy in his cape, but to do so would require more maneuvering and he didn't want to cause any more pain. "Do you have any pets?"

Colton nodded, but just barely. "A dog." His voice trailed on the last word and his head fell back again. Axiom-man adjusted his arms beneath him to angle Colton's head upward.

"I like dogs, too," Axiom-man said. "What's his name?"

"Sh-she. She's a she. She's . . . Belle."

"Belle. That's a pretty name." Axiom-man searched the streets below and adjusted his flight path so he was now directly in line with the hospital. "How about school? What grade are you in?"

Colton cried out. "Arm. My arm!" His broken arm had moved. Axiom-man tried adjusting it into a more comfortable position but Colton kept crying.

"We're almost there, buddy," Axiom-man said. "Just hang on. What grade are you in, again?"

"One. Grade . . ." Colton's head dipped forward.

"Colton, wake up. Colton."

The boy didn't respond.

"Colton!"

The kid's eyes were closed and Axiom-man could barely feel him breathing. He gave the boy a shake, any pain inflicted be damned. "Colton! Wake up!"

Colton didn't respond.

Axiom-man kicked on the speed and went as fast as he could. Colton didn't react from the sudden rush of wind.

*No, no, no . . .* "No, no, no."

Blood sprayed against Axiom-man's costume from the open wound in Colton's leg.

The hospital was just below. A few more seconds and Axiom-man touched down right in front of the ER's doors. They opened automatically and he rushed in. "Help! I need some help!"

The triage nurse and another one came running. They rushed up to the boy and started examining him.

"He got hit by a train," Axiom-man said.

The nurses said something about taking the boy further inside but Axiom-man didn't catch their exact wording.

As they moved through the doors that led into the emergency unit beyond the waiting room, the nurse took her hand off Colton's neck and checked his wrist. She pulled out her stethoscope and tapped it in places across his chest. She put her ear to his mouth then whispered something to the other nurse. A doctor rushed up and she whispered something to him. Tears were in her eyes when she looked up. "I'm sorry," she said. "He's gone. A few minutes sooner and maybe . . ."

Axiom-man's face cracked beneath his mask. He didn't know if the nurses saw the tears glazing his eyes.

He helped them lay Colton's body down on a bed and Axiom-man stood by while they double checked his vitals and the doctor did his own examination.

The way the nurses moved—much slower than if there was a chance of saving Colton—said it all.

"Time of death: two-thirteen," one nurse said. To Axiom-man: "I'm sorry. He had passed even before you came in. Tell us what happened."

Axiom-man relayed the story and let the nurses know if the parents wanted to talk to him, they could. The hospital would just have to call the cops and an officer would be in touch. Once done, he exited the building. Fortunately, Colton had his name and phone number written on his T-shirt's tag. Good on his parents for that precaution.

Standing on the hospital's curb, the regret tore into Axiom-man like a tornado. He shouldn't have slowed down to accommodate Colton's pain. He should've stayed the course and got there as fast as he could no matter what. Even the nurse said a few minutes would've made all the difference. Those few minutes were lost because he had slowed down.

"It's my fault," Axiom-man whispered. "I'm so sorry, Colton. I'm so so sorry."

Axiom-man looked to the sky, its blue and sprinkling of clouds a reminder of being up there with Colton.

Not today.

Today he'd walk.

Flying had suddenly lost its appeal.

## Portraits

Ashton Oz only dealt in original paintings. His paintings.

The same three paintings.

Sort of.

All were done against a background of black oil paint streaked with purple that had a red swirl at the center. One portrait was a zombie—green and gray, with milky-white eyes and purple lips dripping with blood from its last kill. One was a werewolf, with brown, matted fur streaked with silver highlights and eyes so cold and white they froze your soul. The last was a vampire—she was beautiful and sexy, with blonde hair, ruby red lips and sparkling-white teeth. The arc in her lower back pushed up her bust in the front and drove nearly every man wild and made every woman jealous.

Ashton was a staple on the horror circuit and known for his realism in bringing his monsters to life. Those same three monsters, consistently depicted inside of a rusted iron metal cage, their poses varied at each show.

He was constantly asked to make prints of his work, but he was adamant about selling only originals of his creations. It limited his sales volume but didn't limit his sales dollars. The three portraits netted him a solid twelve grand once sold. Not bad for a weekend's work.

Today, Horror Con was coming to a close and Ashton sold the final painting—the zombie—minutes before the buzzer went. He packed up his easels, carried them to his car, and took them home: a quaint little place at the end of the street in a quiet neighborhood. He didn't know his neighbors and they didn't know him. He only left his house for shows and groceries. The rest of his time was spent painting those three monsters.

Ashton took the easels down to the basement and leaned them against the far wall. A fourth easel, draped in black velvet, stood in the middle of his studio. He went over to it and removed the covering. It was a duplicate of the background he always used: black oil paint dripping in purple with that red swirl in the center.

Focusing, Ashton traced his index finger around the red swirl, over and over. He closed his eyes and kept spinning his finger. An hour passed, then two. Off and on he'd open his eyes and when the red paint finally began moving, he picked up the pace, his finger twisting around and around until the crimson swirl grew into a living whirlpool on the canvas.

A hungry groan sounded behind him. He glanced over his shoulder at the zombie in the cage. Then he glanced to the cage beside it. The werewolf. Then he took in a heart-breaking look at the beautiful vampire in the one next to it.

"Time to feast, my friends," he said, and stopped moving his finger.

He went over to each cage and let them out. They moved toward him as one as if to attack, but he knew the spell cast around himself would ensure his protection and direct them toward the swirling painting.

The portal.

With a point of his finger, the monsters entered the canvas one by one. Their dinner would be on the other side in their painted counterparts' locations.

One monster was out for flesh and brains.

The other for the thrill of the kill and meat.

The last for blood.

They'd return when done and he'd paint them anew. Ashton was a wizard with paint, mixing oils and acrylics and potions.

A painting wizard called Oz.

# Under the World

All Anne Billoux could assume was her death triggered the mutation.

Or zombification.

Or vampirification.

It was pitch black and she knew exactly where she was: her coffin, six to eight feet beneath the ground.

She had killed herself by hanging, her last memory dangling by a housecoat rope from a beam in her parents' basement. The last thing she saw was the fading image of her barely-swinging feet before all went dark. Then she woke up here, surrounded by plush lining and, when she pressed up hard against the lining in front of her, the wood on the other side.

Even if she hadn't *really* died, the embalming process would've done her in. Yet here she was, just fine.

She smelled her forearm. It didn't stink of rot nor of any chemical, so that ruled out her having become one of the undead. She felt the same forearm for fur or extra hair in case she had turned into a werewolf, and it was as smooth as it always was. She felt her teeth, thinking maybe she'd find fangs and prove her vampire theory. Instead, they were straight and normal.

Anne pressed her palm to her chest; the steady rhythm of her heart beat beneath her touch, which indicated she was indeed alive. She could think; she was aware. Her mind was clear. Those were indicators her brain was just fine, too. But her heart . . . what was it pumping? Certainly not blood. When embalmed, all natural bodily fluids were drained.

She put the tip of her index finger to her teeth while pressing a bulge of skin together against it with her thumb. She bit down hard and pulled; the immediate sharp pain of the bite as she yanked her finger from her mouth made it throb with pain. She placed her finger on her tongue; warm, coppery blood swarmed her taste buds.

Whatever fluids that had been used on her body had been either flushed out or replaced. She put her hand between her legs to see if she expelled the artificial fluids that way, but instead came up dry.

Was she immortal? Maybe if she was a hundred and five and was still ticking, sure, maybe then she'd entertain the possibility her life was endless. But that wasn't the case. She was only in her early forties, too early an age to consider living forever.

She'd moved back in with her folks after her husband died and used his life insurance money to help take care of them. She didn't want to dwell on the reasons she offed herself, like the parental control on her life despite her doing them a favor. Not right now, anyway.

She pressed up against the casket. It didn't budge nor did she expect it to. The weight of the earth above would ensure its closure and, if the casket was also in a burial vault, there was no way of getting out, and she had no way of knowing if that was the case.

*Air*, she thought. *There's limited air in here.* Eventually she'd die from suffocation, but now didn't know if she'd stay dead.

The throbbing in her finger had abated. She squeezed it, ensuring blood would leak out. She licked it and expected to taste what she had before. This time her tongue ran over a tiny rough surface on the skin.

A scab.

She was healing already.

She wondered if the carbon dioxide level in the casket reached poisoning heights and damaged her lungs, if they'd rejuvenate, too, and she'd be stuck breathing in poison, then dying, then resurrecting over and over again.

Anne clawed at the soft liner beside her, tearing at it until she found the casket's wood on the other side. Her fingers ached and stung from the effort so she gave them a rest. Fifteen or so minutes later, they didn't hurt anymore and she surmised they had healed, too. She checked. They were still rough from her efforts but the pain was gone. Perhaps if she clawed out the side of the casket wooden layer by wooden layer and squeezed through the opening and climbed up through the earth at an angle it'd be less weight upon her and she'd somehow get out. Again, that was if there was no burial vault.

*Can I do anything else?* she wondered. She thought of Axiom-man and his ultra strength. *Maybe . . .*

She pressed as hard as she could against the casket's lid. It didn't move.

"No super strength for me," she muttered. *I'm screwed.*

Clawing out the side seemed to be the only option. She tried, scraping her fingers raw against the wood; her nails broke and her fingers bled. The most she got out of her efforts were the fine slivers of wood that had peeled off the casket. It would take forever just to get through this one spot never mind make an opening she could fit through.

She thought of Axiom-man again and how he could shoot energy beams from his eyes. She thought of Redsaw and how he could do the same from his hands, but how to summon those powers—if she had them— she didn't know. Then she wondered if she could fly.

She focused on her eyes, her hands, and willed them to send forth some kind of energy. Nothing happened. She focused on her body and imagined it rising up the few inches of room she had.

Nothing.

No movement.

But to fly . . .

She tried again, not that flying inside a cramped casket would be of any help, but at least it'd tell her she could do something else special besides rejuvenate.

Her fingers were already void of pain. They would be healed over soon, she supposed. Maybe with patience she could claw through the wood? A round of pain, healing, more pain, healing, over and over until she broke through?

Anne focused on her body.

*Up.*

*Up.*

*Go up.*

She imagined herself rising off the casket bedding and pressing against its lid. Imagined pressing against it so hard she'd push through whatever was on the other side and emerge above the dirt instead of being here underneath the world.

She imagined.

She hoped.

She prayed.

A low rumble drilled into her ears as her body rose and pushed against the casket's lid. A strange scraping and sandy sound began somewhere on the other side of the barrier.

*I'm flying! I'm doing it! I'm*— The rumble sounded louder, and what had to be dirt crunched and moved on the other side of the lid. Her body forced the casket upward and she envisioned the dirt parting as she brought her confines toward the surface.

*I guess there* was *no burial vault,* she thought. Maybe her parents didn't see the point of one. No matter. She was moving. The whole casket was moving. The dirt was moving. The scraping, pebbly and sandy running of coarse earth. Then the sound eased then stopped completely.

*Push!* she thought.

The casket's top and bottom lids burst open and she rose horizontal into the air. The sudden onset of panic kicked in and she flailed her arms and legs as she lost concentration and fell to the ground beside her grave. She lay there, still, and caught her breath.

*What the hell just happened?* She raised her head and looked back over her shoulder. The memorial marker was already installed. For how long it had stood there or how long she had been beneath the earth, it was impossible to tell. Perhaps the air had stayed oxygenated because no breathing had taken place until not long ago.

It was dusk now and the remaining sunlight shone on her name.

ANNE BILLOUX

BORN NOVEMBER 12, 1974
DIED NOVEMBER 12, 2017

OUR LITTLE GIRL. ALWAYS.

There was no snow so she must have been under for six months at minimum.

Six months that went by in a blink of darkness, and now here she was, alive, with the ability to heal and apparently move things with her mind.

137

Reborn.
Telekinetic.
Powerful.
She just didn't know where to go from here.

## Paraphrase

Ronald was born three weeks premature to David and Eleanor Queensvelt, and though those three weeks were still in the premature safe zone, the jaundice caused complications and for two days David and Eleanor thought they would lose the baby. Ronald pulled through, but refused to breastfeed so Eleanor resorted to bottles.

At four years old, Ronald climbed onto the stove just after the burners had been turned off and burnt his palms and knees. He was taken to the hospital and treated.

At six, the family moved to Flin Flon and Ronald spent the next six years climbing the town's rocky hills almost daily. An introvert in grade school, he made only one friend—Graham—who would later commit suicide in his mid-twenties.

In grade seven, Ronald got into his first and only fist fight and lost, but not before going down giving the other guy a broken nose.

At sweet sixteen, Ronald fell in love with Beth Green, but didn't tell her how he felt until graduation. It turned out she had a crush on him, too, and the two dated until they were twenty-one. Beth died in a car accident while driving back to her parents' place after a late shift at the local grocery store.

Ronald started drinking to numb the pain and doubled his daily bottle usage after his father died shortly after from a heart attack. A year later, his mother died of a broken heart.

Samantha came along when Ronald was thirty-one and they were married six months later. One night, she told him to choose between the bottle and her. He chose her, namely because she was barren and he knew he was all she had in terms of family.

Working at the local mine provided for them throughout the years. Samantha ended up being a part-time cashier at the same store Beth once worked. Ronald only went inside the store twice during Samantha's tenure, each visit laden with haunting imagined images of Beth's final shift and the fate that awaited her.

Samantha quit the store at forty-seven. Ronald retired eleven years later at fifty-eight. He enjoyed being the same age as his wife. Reminded him of Beth.

At sixty-four, Samantha fell victim to Alzheimer's and soon Ronald became no more than a stranger. She died at seventy.

When he was seventy-eight, Ronald finally moved out of the house he and Samantha shared all those years to an apartment uptown.

When he turned eighty, he decided he'd had enough of the loneliness and loss and so downed a bottle of Advil and a bottle of gin. Miraculously, he survived. After a shouting match with God about why He let him live, Ronald decided to finish his life, however much longer he had.

Four days after turning eighty-three, Ronald died in his recliner watching the evening news. He had simply grown sleepy, closed his eyes, and finally left this world, his wish granted.

# Delusional?

Lance Davis was plain ol' crazy. He had to be. He was one of those guys who sat at the end of the bar, and if you got close enough for him to notice you, he'd scoot over and start telling you about his life. I know because I was that guy. One of many. And more than once, too.

Everyone at Dave's Bar knew to let Lance keep to himself and let him just stare into his mug of beer and shot of whiskey and leave him well enough alone. But, sometimes, the bar got crowded. And, sometimes, you wanted to sit at the bar and order your rounds head on instead of waiting for a waitress to come by your table. Sometimes you needed to stare into your own beer.

So there I was, Friday night, crawling off a fourteen-hour shift and into a beer glass, sitting next to Lance. The dude was in his late sixties, possibly early seventies. Doesn't matter. Lance was old so, I supposed, I should cut him a little slack if he wanted to ramble. The Lonely Old Man thing.

"You remember what I told you, right?" Lance said. His bright hazel eyes stared into mine. "Trust no one. This world is changing in ways you can't possibly comprehend. Guard up. Everyone is suspect. Everyone is *a* suspect."

"I remember," I said. It was a partial truth, what with Axiom-man flying around and Redsaw causing trouble in ways the world was never equipped to handle. But to trust no one? To give everyone a second glance? A second pondering? I didn't want to become constantly paranoid and live in fear. That's no way to live life, which was hard enough on its own never mind adding guys in capes with frightening powers to the mix.

"Axiom-man made a mistake," Lance said. "He came out to the public. He showed himself. I told you this before: he would've been better off operating in secret, like I did."

There it was. I was waiting for it. See, Lance thought he used to be a superhero back in the fifties and into the early eighties. I asked him once what he called himself and he said he never gave himself a name.

"Codenames are for pansies," he'd said, "guys who crave attention so need to be called something for the papers. I never did that. I stayed in the shadows, the dark, no name. Just a black costume. A simple one. Black suit and tie, full-face black mask, and a fedora. Black gloves, too, because fingers leave fingerprints. But no name. Names give you existence, make you a 'real' person."

I wasn't sure if I agreed with that assessment, but I understood what he was getting at.

"This world's going to bloody hell and nobody's noticing," he said.

I took a sip of my cold beer. "I disagree. I think they are noticing but don't know what to do about it so are looking to others like Axiom-man to handle the problem for them."

"Do you really think the guy's powerful enough to stop what's coming?"

"Which is?"

Lance's voice went down to a whisper. "War. Humans versus—what do they call them now?—metahumans?"

"Well, there's around seven and a half billion of us with armies of various sizes, and only a few of those with special powers." Actually, so far as I was aware, it was just Axiom-man and Redsaw. If there were any others, I hadn't heard of them yet. I found it also strange Lance was telling everyone all this despite his previous assertion heroes operated in secret. Perhaps now, he believed, it wasn't time for secrets. Not for him, anyway.

"They'll come for me, you know," Lance said. "It's inevitable I'll be found out." He took his whiskey back in one go then chased it with a gulp of his beer.

All I did was pressed my lips together and took in the bar. Every seat was taken, the waitresses scrambling about to get drink orders, the bartender barely keeping it together to handle the work they gave him.

"If I was younger, maybe—just maybe— I'd join the fight," Lance said.

"The war?" Couldn't believe I was entertaining this.

"All war. There wasn't a bullet that could stop me, no knife that could pierce this rawhide skin of mine." He showed me his wrinkled and leathery hands as if to prove his point.

Poor Lance. I had gotten other snippets of his life. Divorced early. Second wife died. Two of his kids committed suicide and one disowned him because he kept going on and on about heroic glory days he could never prove. I think he lived in that superhero fantasy of his to salvage what he thought was a waste of a life. I thought maybe—perhaps— I'd do the same if everything had gone wrong for me, too.

Lance signaled to the bartender for another shot. I copied him, raising my finger without meaning to. Wasn't in the mood for anything hard. Oh well.

"Just be careful, son," Lance said. "I've told nearly everybody in here to be careful. Most just laughed. Everyone thinks they're invincible until they're in real trouble. Just wait. You'll see. Things will go haywire and everyone will panic."

A shotgun blast made me jump in my seat and the crowd in the room let out a collective yelp. Two guys in ski masks stood by the door.

"All right, everyone stay where you are and this'll be over real quick!" one of the masked men said.

I looked to the bartender. He already had his hands up in surrender. I looked to Lance. He had his lips around the rim of his glass, sipping back what was left of his beer.

"Don't move!" the other guy in the mask said. He pointed his weapon this way and that.

One of them came up to the bar, the other covering his partner, weapon trained on the room. I knew other guys in the bar were packing and I hoped to God the place wouldn't light up in a gunfight.

"Cash. Now. Quick!" the one gunman told the bartender.

"Su-sure," the bartender said and immediately went for the register.

I saw a couple guys stir in their chairs, reaching into their leather jackets.

*Please*, I thought. *No guns. It'll be a bloodbath otherwise.*

I looked to Lance. He held his empty beer glass aloft, as if inspecting it, then slowly turned it face down on the bar. Once he set it down, he stood from his seat.

"Sit down!" the guy controlling the room said.

Lance didn't say a word.

*Oh no, Lance, don't,* I thought. *You're just a crazy old man. You're gonna die real quick.* I hoped Axiom-man would show up and put an end to this. The doors remained closed. No hero in a blue cape.

"Not kidding, old man. One more step and you're done!" the gunman said.

"Hurry up!" his partner shouted at the bartender.

The bartender scrambled to get all the cash from the register, dropping bills to the floor in his panic.

Lance took that extra step.

The shotgun went off.

Lance's shirt blew apart . . . and he kept walking.

The gunman stood stunned.

I think my heart stopped.

Lance calmly walked up to him and ripped the shotgun from the guy's grasp. He swung it like a baseball bat to the guy's head and the man dropped. His partner turned and fired at Lance point blank.

And Lance still kept walking.

He stepped up to the gunman at the bar and punched him in the nose and kicked him in the shin. He grabbed the man's gun and brought it down like a battle axe to the top of the guy's head.

My heart might or might not have started beating again.

Lance looked back at me; his shirt was blown open, revealing old leathery skin—that was completely undamaged except for some scorch marks from the blasts. He mouthed to me the word "war," then, without looking at anyone else, headed for the door, leaving the rest of us catching our breath.

I was sure my heart started beating again because this time I felt its pulse all the way down into my fingertips.

Lance opened the door and stepped into the night.

Into the shadows.

# Scenarios

Susie walked the street alone. The hole-in-the-wall restaurant she worked at with the crappy pay was only eight blocks from her apartment in a neighborhood, it seemed, the city forgot about years ago. But what more could be expected by a twenty-year-old with no job experience who left home in a rich neighborhood because she couldn't get along with her folks?

The streetlights were dim, barely enough for her to cast her own shadow.

She kept to the sidewalk even though the streets were bare at this hour. At 2AM, all were indoors.

She passed a black mitten on the sidewalk, its wool full of grime and dust. The grime was so thick it looked like it still had a set of fingers in it.

Susie never understood how a single article of clothing could just be laying around. Wouldn't a person notice if a glove fell off their hand? Or, later, if they reached into their pocket to get it only to come up empty? Why leave it? Why not retrace your steps and find the damned thing? Guess people in this area could afford to lose things despite, it seemed, that most could barely afford to keep dinner on the table.

No sooner did her curiosity about the mitten fade did she find a shoe on its side one pace over to the right. It was old with cracked leather. Its shape looked fancy, something higher-end, which was out of place here.

She took a closer look and noticed a pale gray bump topped with dark brown partly sticking out of its top. She squatted down and righted the shoe. Her stomach lurched. The gray and brown sticking out its top—it was a foot.

Still inside of it.

Her first instinct was to bolt and get the hell out of there. Her second was to call 911. As she reached for her phone, she imagined a person violently tripping and falling, snapping the bone above their ankle so badly it shot forth from the skin, nearly severing the foot on its own. Then, in a fit of panic, the person trying to hobble away only to further aid cutting off the foot and losing it altogether.

No blood trailed down the sidewalk so that wasn't case.

Then she thought of *Saw* and someone copying the end in some weird suicide attempt, the blood loss alone being enough to do them in. Why out in public, she didn't know, but, again, no blood around the area. Just the severed foot stuck in a shoe.

The image of a brown truck struck her mind's eye with some crazed psycho behind the wheel and him tossing the shoe out his window as if it was his way of disposing of a chopped-up body with bits and pieces of some poor soul scattered throughout the city.

Susie thought back to the mitten and the caked-on brown grime on it. Was a hand *really* still inside of it? She stood, wanting to go look, but her legs wouldn't let her move. If there was a hand in there, she didn't know what she'd do.

Probably freak out. Perhaps even pass out.

That shoe. That foot.

Her mind wandered to where she watched as a man pinned someone to the ground and sawed away at the person's foot with a hacksaw.

Her mind traveled to a black car pulling up to the sidewalk, two big, mob-like guys coming out and nabbing a person and stuffing them in the trunk only to slam the trunk down while the person's foot still hung out, cutting it off.

*You have to stop,* she thought. *Get up, move on. Call for help.*

The shoe.

The foot.

No blood.

A random body part laying on the street.

A part of her wanted to remove the foot in morbid curiosity; another part wanted to throw up.

*Stop it!*

She stood, turned from the shoe, and spewed chunks of her fries-and-gravy dinner onto the sidewalk. When she straightened, she heard footsteps behind her and in her pukey daze envisioned the shoe hopping toward her.

She needed to call 911.

Susie put her phone in front of her and through teary-eyed vision punched in 9-1—

Arms wrapped around her and pulled her backward. She fell to the ground and landed on her ass, then was forced to lie flat by two gloved hands on her shoulders that pushed down with such force she dropped her phone.

Crimson stains on a rusty knife passed before her eyes.

A low voice spoke and penetrated her soul. "Time to make a pair."

## Daffodil Girl

Bruce stood in the wheat field off the perimeter, a good hundred or so meters from the road, staring at the daffodil. It had no reason to be out here, and despite having had spent long hours combing through the rest of the field, he couldn't find a flower like it—or any other flowers for that matter.

Just a lone daffodil in a wheat field, somehow growing, somehow adapting.

For oh so long.

"Thought I'd find you out here," Janie said, coming up behind him.

Bruce glanced her way and his heart melted at the soft ringlets of her brown hair and the way her purple-and-green flowered dress complimented every inch of her body. Her eyes, bright and golden, stood out even in contrast to the wheat around them.

"Don't know where else I'm supposed to be," he said. "The flower's in bloom again."

"Our flower is always in bloom." She stood tightly beside him and leaned her head on his shoulder.

"I wish you wouldn't do that."

"Sorry," she said, and straightened.

Bruce's heart sank when she did but knew it was the right thing to do. "I keep wondering what went wrong, why we didn't get a chance?"

"There was always magic," she said, "but you fought it."

"No. I gave into it . . . and lost myself to it."

"This field used to be ours. This flower—it's you and me."

Bruce thought back to their picnics here, to their rolling around amongst the wheat, lost in each other's embrace. The kisses, the lingering tongues, the gentle caresses as their hands explored each other's bodies.

"I love you so much, Janie," he said.

"I love you, too. Always have."

"Not 'always.'"

"*Always* since I met you. Love at first sight. It's a real thing though many don't believe in it."

Bruce believed in it, too, because the moment he saw her coming up that high school lawn for the first time, his heart rolled over and he was immediately hers. He'd found himself walking up to her, his legs moving of their own accord, all fear a guy would normally have talking to a girl like her completely non-existent.

Magic.

And when she spoke a simple "Hi," her voice was electric and jumpstarted his life anew. He couldn't place why nor did he care. Later, she confessed, his hello to her had done the same.

"I didn't let you go," he said. "I could never do that."

"But you're trying to. You come out here and find our flower as if wanting to say goodbye but never do."

"I don't know how."

"You'll never find peace until you do."

"What if I don't want to find peace?"

"Then that's really sad. Makes me sad, too."

"Why are you insisting upon this? Why can't we be together."

She curled a brown ringlet behind her ear. "You know that's not possible, not with the way things are."

Bruce's eyes watered. She was right, he knew. The magic was gone.

Stolen from him when she took it with her.

"Fight it," she said, "like you did at the beginning."

"It was a half-second fight."

"Then live in that half-second. Stop coming out and visiting our flower. Neither one of us can move on if you keep doing it."

"This flower is all I have left."

Janie leaned in and kissed his cheek. "Goodbye, Bruce."

"Janie, no." His heart burned.

She bent down and tore the daffodil from the root.

Bruce trembled and found himself bent down as well, the daffodil suddenly in his hand. "Janie . . ."

The wheat field was all that was left.

No flower.

Just like it had been before the day Janie died.

# Holo-writer

Blake sat there in front of his machine, the story going nowhere. He thought the typewriter would do the trick: actually seeing the ink stamped on paper, a visual and progressive motivation to keep things chugging along.

But . . . nothing.

A few measly words, each sentence starting with the word, "Fuck."

The office around him was old, musty, with dust-covered papers and manuscripts and scraps of ideas covering the floor. Blake thought it was hardwood under the pages but he couldn't remember for sure since it'd been so long since he last saw it.

He got up from his desk and lit a cigarette. Old-world tobacco. He approached the window and leaned against it with one arm, the other making sure regular drags were taken off the old smoke. He gazed out onto old town Winnipeg, 1923.

Rachael came up behind him and wrapped her silky arms around his chest. He hadn't heard her enter. She was like that: quiet, sly, but brilliant as well. He enjoyed the warmth of her touch through his button-down shirt.

"Trouble?" she asked.

"Blocked," he said.

"I thought you didn't believe in writer's block?"

"I don't, but this one's tricky."

"What's it about?"

"Saying goodbye to an old flame."

He turned within her arms to face her; she wrapped her hands around the back of his neck.

"Anyone I know?" she asked.

"Yeah. Personally."

"Oh? Who?"

Blake ran his hands down the length of her arms and kissed her deeply, her rich red lipstick coating his lips and tongue. He stroked his fingers through her long, thick blonde hair, and said, "You."

She arched an eyebrow. "Me?"

"Yes. You. I can't keep coming here to work. I have other duties. Ones you wouldn't understand."

Her eyes searched his. "You're married, aren't you."

"Yes. Well, in a way. To a lovely lady . . . but not the kind you think."

To his surprise she didn't let go or throw a tantrum. Instead, she pressed her palms to either side of his head and kissed him good and hard.

"Remember me," she said. "That's all I ask."

He gave her a small grin. "I will."

Then: "What's her name?"

Before he could answer, Rachael slapped him, spun on her heels and headed toward the door.

He furrowed his brow then called out after her, "*Avalon*."

Rachael stopped for a moment . . . then kept going. She had become too real for him. *They* had become too real, and he had been coming here to this typewriter not to write, but to see *her*.

"I'm sorry," he said, the apology meant for the both of them. Blake eyed the glowing red cherry of his cigarette. "Truly. It's for our own good."

Just as Rachael slammed the door, he tossed the lit smoke onto a pile of paper. Soon the pages went up in flame. It spread quickly and the office was engulfed in fire and smoke. Blake stood amongst the flames, the holo-room's safety features ensuring he wouldn't get burned. He could barely even feel the inferno, at least, the one outside his body. Inside, he was alit with passion for Rachael, his heart all hers.

"Fuck," he said. Then, "*Avalon*, end program." The fiery office faded away and he stood in the glowing, blue-walled holo-room.

Captain Blake Pierce exited, then took a step back and lingered at the door right where Rachael once stood. Oh how he loved her, but he loved the *Avalon* more and his romance with his ship would always overrule anything with a holographic girl.

The sirens sounded. Someone had triggered the Red Alert. He'd be needed on the bridge. Blake looked back at the holo-room once more and envisioned the burning office in his mind's eye.

No more time for hobbies and stories.

No more time for love.

He headed to the bridge and wondered if the pain in his heart was worse than whatever alien threat summoned his presence.

There was only one way to find out.

He got into the elo-lift. "Fuck."

# (Re)creation

Peter Parker, bitten by a radioactive spider, received superpowers in return.

Bruce Banner, hit by gamma rays, received monstrous superpowers.

Barry Allen, struck by lightning and crashed through a wall of chemicals, superpowers.

Steve Rogers, injected with the super soldier serum, superpowers.

Fantastic Four, exposed to cosmic rays while on a space mission—superpowers.

And that was just the beginning of the list Curt Maxim made to reinforce the point that, under the right circumstances, superpowers could be obtained.

Curt was eighteen years old, fresh out of high school. Worked as a grocery bagger at Safeway and had no idea what he wanted to do as a career. But he did know one thing: his city was a dangerous place to live and it needed help.

He stood alone in his mother's bathroom, an empty tub before him, the voices in his head always chanting.

"Ha, ha, look at Curt, all covered in yoghurt!" Jake Climbston said. Jake thought himself a football star but never made the team so seemed to take his frustration out on anyone smaller than him.

"You kidding? I hate freckles. Yeah, I said freckles. The ones *you* have," Sheila Langhart said that day Curt asked her to the prom. Boy, was she a knockout. He'd had a crush on her for years.

"Quiet!" Curt said, pressing his palms to the side of his head.

He surveyed the crowded, bottle-covered sink in front of him: mouthwash, WD-40, paint thinner, coffee, milk, pesticide, hairspray, hair dye, whisky, acetaminophen, Robaxacet, shaving cream, and many other things.

Superpowers.

Random occurrences, random mixtures. So far as he understood anyway, especially in the case of Barry Allen.

One by one, he dumped each bottle's contents into the tub. When the mixture grew too thick, he added a bit of tap water, figuring the chemical additions to the city's water would only add to his cause.

"What are you doing in there? Why are you taking so long?" his mother asked through the door.

"Nothing. Taking a crap. Sometimes it takes time."

"Whatever you say."

*Yeah, whatever I say.* He mixed the strange brew with a wooden spoon, in his mind's eye imagining the various molecules from each item connecting, bonding, becoming something they were not before. The concoction smelled awful, but who said becoming super was all rose petals and bubble gum?

Gum.

Curt spat the piece he chewed into the mixture.

He stripped down naked and looked at himself in the mirror. His gut stood out, his mini man-breasts always a source of defeat. Guys his age should be athletic and trim. But his asthma . . .

He snapped his fingers, remembering his inhaler. He dug around in his jeans' pockets on the floor, pulled it out, and sprayed it into the mix until it was empty. Once more, he gave the stuff a stir.

"Time to let it sit," he told himself, again envisioning the bonding of molecules and atoms.

"You'll never amount to anything." Those were his father's words before he skipped out on him and his mom four years back.

"You have to make a decision about your future." His mother's voice. "Can't be a bagger forever. Do that, and you'll be a *begger*."

Curt leaned over the counter, stared at the mirror, and looked himself in the eye. "I'm going to save this city. I'm going to be great. I won't be a begger. I won't be a nothing."

He turned the bathroom lights off, picked up his flashlight, and stuck it between his teeth. Shining the light on the bulbs above the sink, he unscrewed the one closest to the tub. With electrician's tape, he taped down one end of a copper wire deep into the interior of the bulb's housing. He pulled the remainder of the wire close to the tub and laid it down beside it. He turned off the flashlight and fumbled in the dark; he tripped over his clothes on the ground. He smacked his head against the countertop. On his way down to the floor, he turned on the light switch. Somewhere through the daze, there was a knock on the door.

"Curt, what happened? Did you fall off the toilet?" His mother again. "What's that smell? What did you eat?"

"I'm . . . I'm okay," he said, though his head throbbed. He glanced over toward the tub, the tub tilting left then right, growing in and out of focus.

Blood trickled down from just above his eye.

He mouthed the word, "Good." An open wound. Direct exposure to the mixture in the tub.

Curt tried standing, but his spinning head forbade that and the best he could muster was a crawl into the bathtub. He fell over its side and submerged himself in the cold, foul liquid with a splash.

*Soak,* he thought. Goosebumps covered his body and he imagined his pores drinking in the . . . the . . .

All went fuzzy and dark.

Another knock at the door. "Curt! You've been in there an hour. Are you sick?"

It took him a moment to remember where he was. "I'm . . . fine, Mom." He wasn't sure if he thought the words or spoke them, but when she didn't reply, he supposed he had indeed said them and she had left him alone.

He raised his hand out of the liquid. His skin was stained coffee-brown. Curt reached over the side of the tub and found the wire.

"Soon . . . soon I will be . . ." He pulled the wire into the tub with him. The electric current sent him into a spasm head to toe. The alcohol in the brew went aflame.

Heat.

Pain.

Heart pounding in his ears.

His mother suddenly in the bathroom, screaming.

Curt tried to speak, but his mouth was under the liquid and nothing came out.

The booming of his heart. The searing of his skin.

Then silence.

Eyes closed.

Darkness.

\* \* \*

Beneath a heavy blanket in a room smelling of antiseptic, Curt Maxim awoke.

## World War V

Wolfgang Scholz pulled Von Hilder into the ditch the moment Von Hilder got hit. He didn't know Von Hilder's first name and thought it best he never asked the man. In war, it was a good idea not to get too close to your fellow soldier, even if it was with something as simple as a first name.

*Actually,* Wolfgang thought, *a person's name is everything. It's who they are, their identity, their life.*

Von Hilder howled in agony, then said, "How bad is it?"

Wolfgang surveyed the wound. It was in the calf good and deep. The pant leg surrounding it was torn to shreds from the attack; the wound gushed blood.

"It isn't so bad," Wolfgang shouted above the din of gunfire. *Yeah, right.*

Von Hilder gripped Wolfgang hard by the arm. "Don't lie to me. It hurts like hell and I'm afraid to look."

Wolfgang took in the wound again. Blood pooled on the ground beside the leg, and already the surrounding veins were puffy and pressing against the skin's surface, snaking up the leg in gooey worms of pale green.

Von Hilder pulled him in close, face-to-face. "Tell. Me."

"It's not good," Wolfgang said. "I'm sorry."

Explosions rocked the area just beyond the ditch and the wailing cries of men filled the air.

"Take it off," Von Hilder said.

"You could die."

"I'm dead if you don't."

"You could be dead if I do."

Von Hilder's strong hands clamped around either side of Wolfgang's head and he drew him in so close their noses pressed together. "Do it or I'll kill you."

Wolfgang knew what he meant, and simply nodded. He tore off the shredded fabric around the wound, straightened the material, then tied it as a tourniquet just above Von Hilder's knee, hoping to close off the femoral artery. Von Hilder screeched.

Without saying a word, Wolfgang withdrew the machete strapped to his back then firmly took Von Hilder's hand in his. "Be strong, my friend." He wished he had rum or whisky to quickly get his friend drunk to help with the pain, but he had nothing. Even his canteen was empty.

Von Hilder clamped his teeth together and grimaced. After a slight nod, his head fell back and Wolfgang thought he'd already lost him. "Hilder!"

The man didn't reply.

Wolfgang checked for a pulse. It was there. It wasn't too late.

Not yet, anyway.

Just as he was about to sever the leg, one of the enemy appeared at the top of the ditch.

Wolfgang spun to face him and charged him head-on. The enemy opened his mouth in a hissing war cry, but Wolfgang's own scream drowned him out. He plunged the machete into the enemy's heart, withdrew the blade, then plunged it in again.

The enemy dropped.

Another nearby grenade explosion sent Wolfgang flying backward into the ditch. Ears ringing and head spinning, he fumbled for the machete that fell beside him then crawled over to his friend's leg. Von Hilder's entire lower leg was covered in a spider web of infected veins. Wolfgang drove the blade down like a saw just below the knee, the initial deep cut rousing Von Hilder from unconsciousness with a scream. Von Hilder sat up and lashed out at him. For his friend's own good, Wolfgang punched him a few times in the face then gave him a violent right hook across the temple, sending him back under.

Back to work cutting the leg, blood sprayed everywhere as Wolfgang sawed through flesh and bone, the tourniquet not doing its job.

*No matter*, Wolfgang thought. *It might be better this way.*

He sawed through the remainder of flesh, then tossed the severed limb aside. He needed to get Von Hilder out of there.

He sheathed his blade then went to get his friend over his shoulder so he could get him away from the thick of the battle. Von

Hilder's dead weight wasn't easy to sling over his body but he managed to get the man on top of him and started the steep climb up the other side of the ditch and away from the main battleground.

Von Hilder's body jerked and he awoke with a hiss, the sudden movement sending Wolfgang to his knees. *Oh no.* He immediately reached for the tourniquet and let the blood leak out. It might be the only way to save his friend.

The venom.

The vampire venom.

In the bloodstream.

If it hadn't made its way through Von Hilder's entire circulatory system, his comrade might be okay.

Blood poured from the wound in a thick, steady flow. Wolfgang hoped the poison drained with it, but even if the effort was successful, he doubted his friend would make it. At least, he supposed, Von Hilder would die without becoming one of *them*.

Hands gripped Wolfgang's shoulders and it took him a moment to realize Von Hilder was fully conscious. Von Hilder pushed himself off and floated backward in the air and hovered before his formal ally, his eyes bloodshot, his skin ashen.

Tears rimmed the bottom of Wolfgang's eyes. "No . . ." *I'm so sorry, my friend.*

Von Hilder's red eyes bore into him, his severed leg still running blood. The leg would heal, Wolfgang knew, and eventually grow back.

It was too late.

His friend . . . a vampire.

He had failed.

Von Hilder sped through the air toward him, mouth open, fangs sharp. Before Wolfgang could reach for his machete to plunge it into Von Hilder's heart, his friend had already bitten into his neck. The sting of the venom tearing through his veins sent Wolfgang sprawling on the ground.

His fight was over.

His fight . . . in World War V.

# Inferno

The walls burst orange and yellow behind the dark gray clouds of smoke that engulfed the room.

There was a child in here, somewhere, alone.

Maybe dead.

Wes and his crew had been called to the fire on Elm Street over an hour ago when a neighbor saw flames burst forth from the house's windows like soda from a shaken-up can. Now the place had burned right through and was on the verge of collapse.

The hydrant Wes and his crew had tried plugging into was without water pressure and there seemed nothing the City could do about it. Four of the five family members who lived here had been rescued, the dad suffering from third-degree burns as he tried to shield the others from the inferno. But this kid— "Sean!" his mother had screamed—was still somewhere inside.

Wes got low and tried to stay out of the smoke, but the whole house was full of it save for a scant six inches above the floor. The searing heat from the surrounding flames penetrated his protective gear. Sweat coated his body, and his oxygen mask barely kept up.

He tested the first stair leading to the top level. It seemed okay, so he stepped on it and checked the next one. That one was okay, too, so he kept going. The second last step gave way beneath his foot. He tumbled forward onto the burning floor of the top landing.

Somewhere far below: "Wes!" It was Rick, a seasoned firefighter and his best friend.

"I'm fine!" he replied. Carefully, he pressed against the floor to push himself up. The burning wood cracked on the left and broke clean through on the right, making his arm plunge into a fiery hole. He yanked his arm free, regained his footing, and went onward.

He kept low and stepped around the gaps forming in the floor as the top level began to fall in on itself. The crackle and roar of angry flame rushed into his ears. Each door he opened was the gate to Hell; one released a fireball that sent him on his back.

The floor groaned and creaked beneath him.

*Dammit. Get up*, he thought. "Get. Up." He lunged himself forward in a mighty sit-up, the oxygen equipment on his back weighing a ton.

On his feet again, he opened the final door. Flame and smoke burst out; he shielded himself with his forearms.

So. Damn. Hot.

He thought he heard Rick calling for him again but couldn't be sure.

A cry off to the right. Wes looked: a massive pile of toys and clothes and what looked like a chair by a closet. There was no cry for help. Just an anguished wail as the kid trapped behind this makeshift barrier made Wes's heart jump into a panic.

"It's okay. I'm coming to get you," Wes said.

Another wail.

Wes dug his hands into the pile and began pulling away at what had to be a closet's worth of clothes, all packed around a chair that acted like a tent frame. The clothes were ablaze for the first couple feet but had been so densely stuffed they hadn't burned through yet. Interspersed throughout the web of burning clothes were playsets and stuffed animals and building blocks the size of tissue boxes.

*Smart thinking, kid.*

Wes broke through and waved at the smoke. Cast in the orange glow of flame was a boy that looked around seven or eight. Sean. The kid's face was black with soot and he had his hands over his mouth, his shoulders heaving up and down as he tried to breathe. Immediately, Wes gave him the fresh air off the oxygen tank. The kid breathed and breathed the clean air, and as much as Wes wanted the boy to keep going, he had to get him out of here. He took the mask back.

Wood snapped.

The roar of flame sent Wes stumbling into the closet. The boy shrieked as Wes tumbled on top of him. Wes pushed himself off the child, knowing the source of the kid's pain was his hot fire gear.

The doorframe and door collapsed in a heap of fire.

Blocked.

No way out.

*Window.*

Wes stepped over to it and smashed it with his elbow. The glass shattered and smoke billowed its way out. Wes peered over the frame: It was around a twenty-foot drop to the ground.

The floor lit up around his feet.

He stepped through the flame, his own safety be damned.

The boy quickly went up in fire.

"No!" Wes shouted and patted the boy all over, putting him out. He glanced over his shoulder. The window. It was the only way.

Wes ripped off his oxygen mask and unstrapped the tank. Sharp smoke filled his lungs and as he gagged and coughed, he gave the mask to the boy again and got to work removing the tank from his back.

Again, the boy started on fire. Wes patted him out.

*Should I cover him with my body and delay the inevitable?* No, he couldn't. This kid was still alive and still had a chance.

The window.

Fire surrounded them.

Wes took off his coat and gritted his teeth as his clothes caught fire.

"Keep breathing into the mask!" he shouted, wincing at the pain as the inferno stung his skin.

He wrapped the boy in the coat as if swaddling him in a towel.

An explosion rocked the house.

There was no time to waste.

Wes picked up the kid, and through the heavy smoke, barely saw the fear in the child's eyes. Wes's shirt on fire, skin searing, his arms shook from the trauma. Fire swallowed the window's surrounding wall. He took Sean and tossed him through the blaze and out the window. A second after, he thought he should have warned the poor kid but that would have only made the boy tense up and increase the risk of injury even more.

Wes's hair and face lit with flame. He tried patting it out but the room was too hot and he started afire the moment he put himself out. Screaming as the fire took him, Wes prayed the kid landed a safe enough distance outside, broken bones and a few burns the worst case scenario. He should have called Rick. Should have told his friend to catch the boy or be ready or . . . or . . . something. But there hadn't been any time and all he could do was hope he had somehow preserved the boy's life.

The floor gave way and Wes fell through. He hit the level beneath; burning floor landed on top of him. Agony raced through his body as his skin sizzled and popped while he cooked. Sharp and hot smoke filled his lungs and soon he couldn't breathe. Scorching heat ripped through him head to toe, causing his whole body to lock with pain.

Flames roared above.

Smoke flowed in.

Bursts of orange flickered behind the dark gray smoke . . . just as it had when he first entered.

# Dear Mom

*Dear Mom,*

*I'm running away now. My bag is packed. I left some clothes behind so you'd remember me. I took one picture, the one of us on the Ferris Wheel. I don't want to forget you.*

*Thank you for being a good mom to me. Thank you for packing my lunches and seeing me off to school. Thank you for taking me to the zoo. Thank you for my eleven birthday parties.*

*I love you, but it's time to say goodbye.*

*So, goodbye.*

*Your son,*

*Mack*

It wasn't a bad letter. Mack thought it'd be something an eleven-year-old would write. He was always smart so noted his punctuation and spelling were better than most. He just didn't know how to leave the woman he claimed as his mother when he entered her womb and ate the growing fetus within over a decade ago, using its genetic material as a blueprint for his disguise so he could covertly enter the world.

Eleven years on Earth.

Eleven years recording as many lifeforms and behavioral patterns as he could. Eleven years of steady observation and learning.

He remembered everything. Every cartoon episode. Every eavesdrop from his bedroom door while his parents watched the news. Every comic book. Every newspaper his father daily discarded. Every computer game with colorful characters. Every ounce of Google he was able to surf at night while his parents slept.

Eleven years of intake.

Mission complete.

Mack stood by the railway tracks and waited. He thought of his mom and the inevitable tears in her eyes when she read his note. He thought of his father trying to remain strong for her. Mack was their only son. He had rendered his poor mother barren when he infiltrated her womb that night long ago. His parents tried for years to have more kids despite being told it was impossible.

Mack saw the train down the track.

He waited.

It got closer.

*Dear Mom,* he thought, *I'm going to break your heart one more time. Dear Dad, you need to be brave. Do it for her. Do it for the woman you love.*

The train sounded, obviously seeing him. Mack jumped onto the track and ran toward the giant metal machine. The train blew its horn. Mack ran faster.

*Dear Mom, this is the only way we can both be free. You will eventually heal after thinking I'm dead, but don't worry, I won't really die. I will think of you often and carry your memory just as you will carry mine.*

The train plowed into him, splattering his body in a starburst of flesh and bone.

Snartligylin's bone-white semi-transparent form spun out of his mortal housing and flew into the air, the droning of the train's horn still sounding below.

The headline would read: LOCAL RUNAWAY KILLED BY TRAIN, he knew. But it was the only way. Death, though grievous, brought closure. Snartligylin thought this would be the best way to preserve his parents' hearts instead of merely disappearing and forcing them to wonder for the rest of their lives what happened to their son.

*Dear Mom, I love you.*

*Dear Dad, I love you, too.*

Snartligylin broke through the atmosphere and detected the cloaked starship next to the moon.

He headed toward it.

It was time to report and she would be happy to see him.

*Dear Mom, my captain and true giver of life,* he thought, *I'm coming home.*

## Burnt Out

*His time was coming to a close.*

Peter Fox wasn't sure how to start his autobiography, but that one line seemed appropriate.

Because it was true.

Peter's time *was* coming to close and he wasn't sure if that was a metaphor for something professional or personal. His writing career was average. Above average, actually, in that he'd written over forty books in the same amount of time it took most writers to write seventeen, but he was also below average, he knew, in terms of income and stardom. The forty-plus books didn't earn him a heck of a whole lot month in and month out, and what made it worse was he knew there were guys out there making a killing off a handful of titles.

But he'd never been in publishing for the money. Oh, sure, in the beginning there was a dreaming phase of big advances, a giant house, and a few cars. Later, though, he learned those kinds of things were the exception not rule. Still, he tried, and wrote book after book, trying to make his mark in a crowded industry. Tried to make a name amongst a sea of others.

He was partially successful.

It wasn't that his work was awful. The reviews came back positive eight times out of ten. It was just he couldn't seem to surface above water level and surf the wave of fortune and glory.

All he did was write. All he did was pour his heart out on the page through the veil of fiction.

All he did . . . was lose everything and everyone—including himself—in the process.

Now, life consisted of fitful sleeps on some nights, exquisitely lengthy dreamfests on others. Alcohol, caffeine, and nicotine saw him through the day. So did copious amounts of quetiapine, clonazepam, and citalopram. So did muscle relaxers and painkillers.

It seemed he had a liver of steel. He'd hoped after all this time of pouring himself out and taking all those stimulants it would finally catch up with him. Instead, they seemed to keep him going, fueling more words amidst the heartbreak of losing his family and always seeming to fall short of the mark despite how much work he put forward.

Yet . . . the readers—the small audience he had—wanted more, so he had to keep going, keep fighting, keep the depression and anxiety at bay.

He had to live in his head and stay there because any person or thing outside of it didn't give two shits about him as a person.

He hated this world.

Hated what he'd become: an angry, drug-and-alcohol-fueled writer who only wanted to take people on adventures with his work. Who only wanted a life like the ones he'd written about. But that life never came. All he had was pain and a heartbreak story of losing his wife and kids through divorce.

All he had were daily battles to draw more and more people to his work while at the same time producing even more work to draw them to.

Peter prayed and hoped the drugs and alcohol would finally do their job. Would finally be too much. Would finally put an end to his miserable existence. Writers were more successful when they were dead anyway so death seemed the next logical step in taking things to the next level.

Peter looked at the pill bottles, the whisky, the cigarettes, and decided his autobiography would end the same way he opened it: *His time was coming to a close.*

# Bar Fight

The fight broke out at Dave's Bar a little after 12:30AM.

Selena was alone. After trying to go to bed early and tossing and turning for a couple of hours, she hoped she'd have something on hand in her apartment for a nightcap. She didn't, and a sudden craving for pecan whisky took over so she threw on her coat and boots and headed to Dave's. She figured between the walk there, a shot or two, and the walk back, she'd be good and tired and fall asleep no problem.

It was on her second shot of sweet pecan whisky did the guy sitting on the stool next her get a wooden chair to the back of his head. What he did or whom he pissed off, she didn't know. All she knew was the sickening smack of his forehead slamming into the bar top, the glazed look in his eyes as he tried to regain some semblance of composure, then the thick thud of a large fist clocking him across the face and sending him sprawling to the floor.

Selena took in the assailant: about six-five, a solid two-eighty, wearing blue jeans and a thick plaid jacket that made him appear even bigger. The handful of scars that crisscrossed his face told her this wasn't the attacker's first rodeo. One scar ran up his forehead and all along the bald patch on the top of his skull while the remainder of his long black hair sat

182

scraggled on his head in a terrible skullet. All he had to do was point a thick finger at the bartender to buy the man's silence.

He caught Selena looking at him. "What?"

"Nothing," she said, then double checked that her shot glass was empty. Too bad. She could go for a third.

"Good it's nothin'," Skullet said then turned and walked away.

Selena looked at the guy on the floor. The poor sap. Whatever he did, it didn't deserve a public humiliation like that.

"Well, maybe not nothing," Selena said.

Skullet stopped and turned around. "What's that?"

The place went quiet.

"Oh nothing," Selena said. "Just some dude with a bad haircut causing trouble."

Skullet squinted. "You're lucky you're a lady or you'd get something, too."

"From you? Puh-lease. I'd never want to 'get it' from you."

Skullet took a step toward her and one of his buddies stopped him with a hand to the arm. "She's not worth it, man," the guy said.

Skullet pressed his lips together.

"Naw, let him come over here. I am worth it, believe me," Selena said with the sexiest grin she could muster despite sex being the furthest thing from her mind.

Skullet came over to her. "What do you want, baby?"

"I'm easy to please."

"Tell me," he said, though it was clear they were talking about two separate things.

"Just your face eating my fist."

"Mmm . . . I see. It's like that, eh? Freaky. Nice."

"Mmhmm."

Skullet leaned closer. So did Selena. Just as her cheek brushed his, she hooked two fingers under his chin, digging deep into the soft flesh. She pushed up so hard she knocked his head back. A second later, she was on her feet, and the moment Skullet righted himself, she push-kicked him into the table behind. He landed flat on his back, smashing the glass mugs of those sitting there. Quickly, Skullet's cronies turned toward her and made a charge. There were a half dozen of them. Selena ran in between them and kicked one then did a spinning back kick into another. One guy came in from the side with a wide right hook. She ducked then gave him an uppercut before doing a turning kick to his knee and sending him to the floor.

Sensing someone behind her, she did a spinning back fist and cracked the guy's cheekbone. Another came in and he received a swift kick to the nuts. The moment he doubled over, she brought her heel down in an axe kick to the back of his neck. The guy flattened. She ran on top of him and did a flying side kick into another dude about to lunge at her with a knife.

She got near the door.

Voices shouted . . . then chaos reigned, the whole place erupting into a brawl. Fists connected with faces and stomachs while other guys were picked up and tossed over shoulders.

A beer bottle flew at her; she dodged to the side and it shattered against the wall behind her. She didn't know who threw it.

To the side, an unmistakable click as a switchblade snapped open. The big black dude swung in with the knife. Selena caught his arm and grabbed his wrist and twisted his limb into an arm lock, forcing him to drop the blade. She brought her knee up into his face twice then used her hold on his arm to spin him around and kick him into the chaotic crowd.

A dart pierced her shoulder. She yanked it out then threw it back into the crowd, not caring who she hit.

Skullet appeared beside her and got a shot into her ribs. She took the blow then fired back with a crescent kick across his chin then, as his neck cranked to the side from the impact, she came in from the other side with the same kick but with the opposite leg. Skullet's head jerked the other way and she could only imagine the strain on his neck. She grabbed him by the back of his collar and dragged him over to the ATM and sent his face into the screen.

Looking back at the bar, half the place was already either unconscious or had quit. A few guys threw fists in the corner. One chick beat her hands against a guy's back while his attention was on someone else.

Skullet groaned and started to pull away from the machine. Selena kicked his head back into it and he slumped to his knees and didn't move.

A rush of dizziness from the adrenaline dump came over her.

Glass shattered somewhere in the room. Wood cracked. Men beat on each other. Women beat on other women.

Sirens sounded far away, somewhere on the other side of the door.

Selena took her bow and headed out from Dave's.

Sometimes all you needed was a drink and a good old-fashioned bar fight.

# Dragonfly

Talia's skin was so smooth, so warm, so soft. Every touch Darin gave her was like touching glass. She rode him smooth and even, sending electric waves and pulses of pleasure throughout his body. Her moans told him she enjoyed this, too. Soon, her breathing quickened and small gasps of delight escaped her lips. Darin groaned as he felt himself getting closer to climaxing. Talia picked up her speed but still kept her pace strong and even. He pulled her in close and kissed her hard, then ran his lips across her cheek, down her neck, along her shoulders and lingered on the blue and green dragonfly tattoo just above her triceps.

Warm skin.

Oh, she felt so good. So amazing.

That skin. That smell—rich with strawberries and vanilla.

Talia pulled him in hard and quickened her pace, her moans of ecstasy turning him on and making him climb that mountaintop faster. She bucked and let out a loud cry, her hips locking for a moment before releasing and continuing her movement. Darin drove into her but still let her keep control. Soon, a shockwave of pleasure ignited between his legs and he released within her, pulse after pulse of ecstasy. Talia slowed her pace and eased him down off the ledge, running her hands across his chest as if to slow his speeding heart.

"Oh my gosh," he whispered in her shoulder, then buried his face into her neck. He kissed her gently there before she guided his lips to hers.

With a push of her fingers, she tilted his head back and kissed his neck as her hips still moved. Her tongue felt incredible along his neck as she licked and kissed him. He ran his hands up and down her smooth back before gripping her backside and slowing her movement so she barely moved at all.

After catching his breath, he whispered, "I love—"

Sharp pain cut deep into the side of his neck. He shouted. The pain dug deeper, and the sharp sensation told him one thing: she was biting him. What had to be dagger-like teeth moved faster and faster as they tore through his flesh. Darin tried pushing her off but she clamped onto him with an iron grip, her fingers suddenly feeling like claws taking full hold of his skin and muscle. Blood sprayed all over the side of his face and hers, turning his vision red and blurry.

His neck. The pain. The scraping and tearing as she chewed through.

"Stop," he wanted to say, but all that came out of his mouth were gushes of blood.

He beat on her back with his fists then was suddenly repelled when some kind of sticky mesh stuck out of her flesh. Through the red blur—wings. Enormous, insectoid wings.

Darin's head flopped to the side, and in a series of loud crunches, she gnawed through what could only be his vertebrae.

Talia.

Her skin.

Oh, her skin. Smooth and slick with blood. His hands and arms went limp as she cut his spinal cord.

In a way, the relaxation felt good.

She'd felt so good.

Talia.

# Succumb

"You know, I can't keep doing this," Matt said. "Please, I beg you, let me go."

"You know what will happen if I do that," the man in the black shroud said.

Matt had never seen the man's body, only the rough and tattered dark, hooded cloak that merely revealed a gaunt face with sunken eyes.

"No more. I can't take it anymore," Matt said. "No more!"

"Then your family dies."

"Please, let them go. I'll do anything."

"That's what you said after I first took them. And I gave you your 'anything.'"

The *anything*.

The nightmares, the tormenting dreams, the torture so real Matt swore he was awake and not asleep when it happened.

Three years of nightly torment. Three years of not knowing if the hooded figure told him the truth and if his family was really alive. His wife, Allison, perfect in every way and then some. His sons, Matt junior and Michael. Three long years of not seeing their precious faces. Three long years of them growing up somewhere without their father and at the mercy of a madman.

"I . . . I can't. My head. My heart," Matt said. "Do something else to me."

"Night is when I come. You know this, and you know the punishment for trying to stay awake."

Matt did. He remembered trying to outsmart the dark man with energy drinks and copious amounts of coffee and trying to get his doctor to give him something that would boost his energy levels so sleep would be minimal. It worked, but for a short time. It was once the stuff wore off and sleep overtook him did Matt find himself hanging from chains with this boogeyman cutting into him with a rusted machete. With him sawing and chopping off limbs only for them to grow back so Matt would suffer the agony all over again. The penalty lasted two months.

Lesson learned.

But there was one thing Matt knew: the boogeyman needed him. He was like a drug to the hooded figure, gave him his fix of nightly torture. Out here in the waking world, the boogeyman couldn't be satisfied, it seemed. He needed the land of dreams to become the terror he was.

Needed someone to comply.

Not anymore.

Matt decided he'd leave the room and quietly off himself. Then, and only then, would the boogeyman lose his source.

"I know your thoughts," the boogeyman said. "I also know you thinking killing yourself will stop me. Listen carefully: if you die, they die. Your family will be gone, and an entire legion of my kind will ensure they suffer until their last breath. They will be tormented while awake, but when they sleep and give in to the darkness of pain, they will awake in our world and suffer tenfold. A hundredfold. You are mine, Matt. *They* are mine."

The hooded figure came over to him. He outstretched a bony hand, and try as Matt might to swat it away, he couldn't raise an arm to do so. The trance was already beginning.

The boogeyman touched his forehead. "Sleep, human. Sleep, and do this 'anything' you promised."

Darkness closed in around Matt's vision and when his sight returned, fire surrounded him and his body alit with searing agony.

A pit.

He was in some kind of pit. His flesh crackled and burned and he fell to his knees. Screaming, he tried crawling to the pit's edge only for the boogeyman who stood on its ledge to push him back down with a hot iron spear, one that plunged into his shoulder and ripped into his flesh.

"No . . . no . . ." Matt whispered, then gritted his teeth from the pain.

"Yes, Matt, yes," the boogeyman said. "Come crawl again and let the cycle repeat."

Matt's burning limbs moved under the boogeyman's spell. He crawled. He climbed. The spear plunged in. He fell back down.

Over and over and over, Matt's screams overriding the roar of flame.

## The Jump

Tina stood on the edge of the cliff and looked down. It was easily a hundred-storey drop, if not more, one that ended on jagged boulders with sharp trees jutting out from in between them.

*I can't do this,* she thought, but there was no other way to get to the other side of the life she now led. Master Bram even said so.

"You're special, Tina, just like the others," he had said. "You deserve more. *You* are more, but no one in your life has ever seen it. No one but me."

She knew his words were true. Master Bram's words were always true and his teachings irrefutable, especially the one about humanity living with a limited mindset and not seeing what could be beyond their meaningless little lives.

Master Bram had given her a home and love along with five other teenage girls. The other four, they had already jumped, already proven their worth to their master.

Proven their trust.

Now, those girls had moved on to greater things. Bigger things. Better things.

"The only way to be free of the life you now live is to step off this cliff and join the others," Master Bram said. "Have no fear, child, for I will be right behind you."

It was hard to read his expression beneath the big brown hood that covered his face. It was the same cloak he wore when they lit the candles at night and prayed for revelation to what he and the girls really were.

"We go one by one, but we do this together," he said.

Tina peered down over the ledge. The rocks and trees suddenly looked even sharper. "What if I can't do it?" she asked. "What if it doesn't work?"

"My dear child, I have always told you the truth, have I not? The others believed and look what happened—they were enlightened and now soar through the clouds, becoming what they were destined to be. I searched the earth for you. You were once lost but now found. Trust me. It will be all right. Have faith."

Tears leaked out of the corners of Tina's eyes. All she could do was nod and take a deep breath, though it did little to still her speeding heart or calm her rubbery limbs.

Master Bram moved behind her and placed his hands on her shoulders. He nudged her closer to the ledge. Her toes curled over the edge of it but she stopped herself, pressed back against him.

"Not yet," she said. "I'm not ready."

"You are, my child. You are . . . but you must do this on your own. Just believe. Be free."

Freedom. That was the promise. Freedom from this world to become something more.

Tina closed her eyes and took another calming breath. Her heart slowed a little. She thought of the other girls. She thought of Master Bram. She thought of the truth imparted over the past six months.

Her heart became still.

Tina opened her eyes . . . and stepped off the ledge.

Her body plunged toward the jagged rocks below. In seconds she would be set free. In seconds, it would all be over and she'd join the others in the sky. In seconds . . . her back split open, the muscles tearing and bones breaking, sending a jolt of pain throughout her body that made everything lock up and bright white stars dance along her vision. From just behind her, a sudden whoosh as wings blew out of the back of her body.

The ground rushed up to meet her.

Her wings flapped of their own accord and her descent slowed. She soared over the rocks and trees and ascended to where her friends waited for her in the sky, the exhilaration of flight setting her spirit free and removing her from the mere human she once was.

She glanced over her shoulder. Master Bram had removed his cloak, revealing a pair of massive black wings with shimmering feathers. He took off from the cliff's ledge and joined them in the sky, each flap of his dark wings sending golden dust into the air.

He joined them, just like he had promised, and had set them free.

Master Bram always told the truth.

# Thief

Robin sat perched high up in the tree. Even after all these years, he still had a thing for heights and its ability to let you see everything. So many years. So many trees.

Wagon nineteen hundred and six was not far down the well-worn path through Sherwood Forest. Robin had killed countless men in his lifetime, but for some reason kept track of the number of wagons that were the source of his bounty. They ran through Sherwood once a week, sometimes more. With a slight grin, he thought back to better days when he had his men by his side. Now, it was just him and Tuck left, and the old friar was no longer good in a fight. He was no longer good for anything other than saying prayers and, on a good day, ministering to Robin. The friar had denounced his order over a decade ago, approximately twenty years after the Sheriff of Nottingham's reign of terror had come to a bloody end. The new threat was Rome and how the church in Nottingham was no longer a place for God but for greedy men who consolidated power in His name.

That was this wagon. More money headed for the cathedral. The priests claimed it was to adorn it as a place worthy of the God of the universe, but the amount of money coming in didn't reveal itself in new stonework or paintings or even sacred elements for mass. Instead, a covert operation at night to investigate the cathedral showed Robin the money was spent on the priests' quarters and women.

None of it aided the poor except for an annual sharing of food.

It was a new Holy War now, one man against the greatest religious institution in the world. The god Rome worshipped wasn't the same as the one Robin kept in his heart.

"Lord, be with me," he whispered and produced his bow. He armed it from his quiver and readied his shot.

The wagon drew closer. One driver, four others on horseback, two on each side. There was likely two or three more within the wagon guarding the treasure.

Carefully aiming his shot, his old eyes not what they used to be but his hands and arms filled with decades of skill, Robin let the first arrow fly. It clipped the driver's helmet across the nose piece, the force of the arrow knocking him from his position.

Robin took hold of the rope already in place and swung down. The moment his feet touched the forest floor, he withdrew his sword from its sheath and slashed at the first man on horseback, running the blade across his belly. It didn't penetrate the armor but was enough to knock him off the saddle. Robin sliced through the horse's legs, using the attack as a distraction while the first soldier got to his feet. Robin charged him and went for the bare skin beneath the helmet's metal brow, penetrating his blade into the man's brain. Withdrawing his sword, he spun to meet the driver who had gotten to his feet. Robin blocked his bladed attack and did the same to him, cutting into his skull and ending him.

The remaining three men dismounted and charged him. Robin slammed his blade into the ground as if staking his claim on the wagon. Bow back in hand, he shot two of the soldiers in the face, leaving just one more to tangle with. The man came in, his sword bearing down. Robin dodged, then pulled his sword from the ground. The blades clashed, and in a flurry of movement, Robin used the aggressive moment to get behind the soldier. He slashed at the back of the man's knees then brought the handle up to knock the man's helmet off. He drove his sword down into the man's head like a spear, lodging it so deep he had to use his foot for leverage to pull it out.

Two more soldiers appeared after a creak of metal.

*The interior guards,* Robin thought.

He blocked another swing of a sword then kicked the man in the face. He met the other soldier's blade, shoved him away, then faced the other one again. Robin dropped to his knees, his sword on the ground beside him. He pulled his bow, loaded it, and shot an arrow up the man's nose, deep into his head. Back on his feet, he ran around the rear of the wagon and ensured no other soldier was inside, then popped up on the opposite side of the wagon as his opponent and sent three arrows his way. One in the throat, another in the face, one in the chest.

Quickly, Robin closed the wagon's rear door, grabbed his sword, and hopped in the driver's seat. With a quick snap of the reins, he sped the wagon further down the trail and away from the fallen men and the other horses.

Heart beating so hard his chest grew tight, shortness of breath came on.

*A little farther,* he thought. He veered the horse off the path then pulled on the reins. The wagon came to a halt. As fast as he could, he rounded the back of the wagon and opened its doors, the chest within no doubt weighing a hundred pounds.

No matter. His old body was used to the strain.

He had to stop for a moment and regather his breath before hoisting out the chest and lugging it to a drop spot further into the forest, well away from the wagon.

Robin covered it with branches thick with leaves and would come back for it later after nightfall.

As he left the site, the excitement of the moment caught up with him and his old joints gave out and he fell to his knees.

*Just a little farther,* he thought. *Please, Lord.*

He was not far from camp.

His chest tightened and it suddenly felt like a horse had him underfoot. His limbs tingled and his head spun.

"No," he said. "That couldn't have been the last one."

Robin quickly found himself face down in the dirt. *No.*

Time passed. Minutes or hours, he wasn't sure. Then someone grabbed him from behind. Robin tried to turn and fight, but couldn't find the strength.

"Easy friend," the hoarse voice said. "This is not over yet."

*Tuck.* "Thank you, Lord."

Robin did his best to aid the old man in helping him to his feet.

"I saw you fall. A vision," Tuck said.

"Thank you," Robin said. He faltered in his steps.

"We will get you back to camp and rest," Tuck said, "then tomorrow, distribute the bounty."

Still light-headed, Robin said, "We will. This war isn't over. The God of Israel will prevail over the god of Rome."

# Extermination

It was a pitiful planet—Earth—one full of lifeforms that didn't deserve to be there.

The Glorw had been monitoring the third planet from the sun for several decades, each one that passed proving more and more this world's inhabitants were nothing but parasites, parasites with two motives: consumption and destruction.

These "humans," as they called themselves, used resource after resource, some natural, some artificial, in an effort to further their race but only to ultimately bring about their planet's end. Whether they knew or not was unknown. Garbage and filth riddled the planet's lands and waters. Where once stood beautiful forests now stood structures of concrete and steel. Unlike the Glowr, whose technology was organically-based, everything on their world alive and crossbred to make new things, these humans destroyed their planet to make things more suitable to their liking. And while true there were many pragmatic purposes to almost everything the humans had created, it always came at a common cost: the end of life. Something always paid the price for the parasitic race's expansion. Plants, creatures, the Earth itself—they all suffered so this so-called more intelligent and dominant species could flourish.

Chief Tornmew, main supervisor of the ship, the *Hencanen*, was summoned to Earth when the Glowr's planetary monitoring system notified them the planet was dying. The Universe itself was a living organism, giving forth life across the cosmos, forming planets and species to fill the void of space. However, the occasional planet would begin to rot because the lifeforms that evolved there ended up destroying the planet piece by piece.

These humans were of that ilk, though Chief Tornmew knew humans considered themselves kings of the Earth. It was only humanity's intelligence that made them so, certainly not their physical abilities. There were far more powerful species on Earth that would wipe out the humans if they knew how. Now, humanity wiped out sources of life every chance it got all in an effort to advance itself.

Even today, there were efforts to transcend the human body and merge human and machine. The humans thought they could live forever by transplanting themselves into artificial bodies and connect their consciousness to what they dubbed the "Internet."

This would only lead to more loss of life.

Earth had fallen.

Chief Tornmew nodded to the soldier beside him. The soldier flicked the switch, and an enormous laser canon emerged from the *Hencanen*. Another switch, and a thick beam of red light shot forth, penetrating Earth's core.

Seconds later, the planet exploded, debris shooting in all directions like the explosion of a star.

Parasites exterminated.

It was time for the Universe to spawn something new.

## About the Author

**A.P. Fuchs** is the author of many novels and short stories. His most recent efforts of putting pen to paper are *The Canister X Transmission: Year Three*, *Axiom-man Episode No. 3: Rumblings*, and *Mech Apocalypse*.

Also a cartoonist, he is known for his superhero series, *The Axiom-man Saga*, both in novel and comic book format.

Fuchs's main website is **www.canisterx.com**

Join his free weekly newsletter at **www.tinyletter.com/apfuchs**

CPSIA information can be obtained
at www.ICGtesting.com
Printed in the USA
BVHW071132240922
647890BV00002B/97